AT
THE
WATER'S
a novel
EDGE

OTHER BOOKS AND BOOKS ON CASSETTE
BY ANNETTE LYON

Lost Without You

AT THE
WATER'S EDGE

a novel

Annette Lyon

Covenant Communications, Inc.

Cover image © Digital Vision/Gettyimages

Cover design copyrighted 2004 by Covenant Communications, Inc.

Published by Covenant Communications, Inc.
American Fork, Utah

Printed in Canada
First Printing: March 2004

10 09 08 07 06 05 04   10 9 8 7 6 5 4 3 2 1

ISBN 1-59156-927-1

DEDICATION

This book is dedicated to Mike, Melanie, and Michelle, with whom I have shared so much, including parents, Finnish heritage, linguistic dinner conversation, cracked-wheat cereal, matching travel outfits, a love of the gospel, and so much more.

I love you guys.

ACKNOWLEDGMENTS

I must thank my editor Angela Colvin for her help and patience as I learned the ropes last time and for her continued support. As always, my husband Rob has been a rock in supporting my writing. Many people read and contributed to this book in its various stages—Michele Holmes, Lu Ann Staheli, Heather Moore, Shauna Andreason, Carol and Ann Lastowski, and Staci Call.

My parents, Mel and Anne Luthy, made sure memory served me right in the details about Finland.

Thank you all—it is a much better story because of you.

CHAPTER 1

"I'm sorry, Annela," Oskar said, sounding anything but apologetic. He sat in his easychair, eyeing first his cigar and then his daughter. "But you can't come back home. You're a grown woman now."

"It would be temporary," Annela said from the couch, trying to convince him. "Just until I could find another place to stay. I'd be on my own again before you knew it."

His right eyebrow arched. "You don't even have a job."

Annela pursed her lips tightly. They had been over this before. She had been laid off from her intern position at Nokia three weeks ago. With the economy in a depression, jobs were hard to find, but she was looking. "I'll find a job. Soon. If you like, I can pay rent while I'm here. I've still got some savings in the bank."

Oskar raised both eyebrows. "If you have money for rent, why do you need to move here? Why don't you stay at your apartment with Tommi?" A look of comprehension dawned on him. "Unless the two of you aren't getting along." He smiled with amusement. "What did you do? It must have been pretty bad if you've upset him while he's out of the country."

Annela rubbed her forehead with one hand. She reached out to touch his knee, then pulled back. "Father, please. This has nothing to do with Tommi. He doesn't know I'm leaving yet." Tommi had been in Stockholm setting up a new location for his restaurant for the past three weeks. He was supposed to have been gone for another week, but surprised her with a phone call that morning saying they finished early and he would return today. Annela had thought she'd have another week to get this all settled.

Oskar leaned forward and pushed his cigar into the ashtray on the coffee table beside him. Clasping his hands together, he said, "All right. Let's get to the point then. If this isn't about you and Tommi, what *is* it about?"

Annela swallowed hard. Of course she would have to tell him, but she had nursed a little hope that she could avoid it for a time. "I've decided . . ." Her voice was scarcely audible.

"Speak up, girl. You've decided what?" His voice rose a notch.

Annela glanced at her father, then back at her hands. She held onto the handle of her purse a bit tighter, knowing her father's tone all too well. The same panic she'd felt a thousand times as a child washed over her, and her heart pounded in her throat.

"I can't live with Tommi anymore because . . . because he's not ready to get married and . . . I'm going to be baptized."

"You're going to *what?*"

Annela spoke a little louder. "I'm going to be baptized, sir. Become a Mormon."

He stood and yanked at Annela's arm to pull her up too. He raised a hand, and Annela flinched, expecting to be struck as her mother had been so often.

"Oskar, don't!" The plea came from his wife, Helena, who had just entered the room.

He whirled around to face her. "This is none of your business, woman! You stay out of it." He turned back to Annela, face bloodshot with fury. He pointed his finger at her, jabbing the air for emphasis. "I refuse to live with a Mormon. The second a drop of baptismal water gets on you, you are dead to me."

Annela steeled herself. "Father, this is something that will make me happy. Don't you want happiness for your own daughter?"

He shook his head back and forth, the veins in his neck popping out. Annela took a step back, nearly tripping on the couch behind her.

"No child of mine would join up with those pagans." He didn't yell. But his voice was filled with such venom that her knees shook.

The lock on the apartment door turned, and sixteen-year-old Kirsti came inside. "I'm home," she said, tossing her book bag onto the floor. She unzipped her jacket, then paused when she recognized the tension in the room. "What's going on?"

"Your sister has decided to leave our family," their father said, looking Annela straight in the eyes.

"Not really," Helena added quietly. "She's trying to live by a new set of values."

"You're defending the little tramp?" he bellowed. Helena clutched the door frame as he went on. "As if our values are somehow inferior? As if we're not good enough for her?"

Kirsti sat on the back of the couch and watched. Annela envied her sister's calm. Kirsti could do no wrong in their father's eyes. It didn't matter what she said or did, so she had no need to worry. "Let me guess," she said to Annela, then popped a piece of gum into her mouth. "You're going to be a Mormon."

"I don't want that word ever spoken in this house again!" Oskar grabbed Annela by the arm so tightly she choked out a cry. The smirk on Kirsti's face evaporated. He dragged Annela to the front door, opened it, and shoved her out of the apartment. "Get out." He slammed the door in her face, sending vibrations and hollow echoes bouncing off the apartment building walls.

Annela took a deep breath to stop the shaking in her body. She gripped the handrail and headed down the stairs.

Before she reached the outer doors she knew exactly where she was headed. Not back to her apartment. She glanced at her watch. Tommi's plane had landed over an hour ago, so he would be back home any minute. She was grateful that he'd insisted she not change her schedule to meet him there, since it was on such short notice. Instead of going home she decided to go to the beach for refuge.

She hadn't taken more than two steps outside before the crisp wind of the Finnish spring hit her. Her coat was in her parents' apartment, and she couldn't very well return to retrieve it. At least she had been holding her purse when her father exploded. She reached into it and turned off her cell phone. Tommi might try to call when he got in, wondering where she was, but she needed time alone right now. Just for a few minutes.

After that she'd call him and take the bus back to the apartment. She'd make his favorite dinner, then tell him she was moving out. But to where? She still wished she could have had the details figured out before giving him the news.

Tommi would be upset when she told him—understandably. But they both knew he wasn't ready to commit to marriage, and since she was determined to be baptized, there was no other option but to leave. It had been a blessing that Tommi hadn't been around since her decision to be baptized almost two weeks ago.

She would have to sleep on the couch for tonight. Then she would go to a hotel. She could afford a few nights at one, probably not long enough to find a new apartment. But she would cross that bridge when she had to. She harbored the hope that Tommi would continue taking the discussions when he returned. He missed the first one, but had been there for the next two. Maybe if he saw the missionaries again he would get baptized and want to get married. But in the meantime . . .

Annela walked down the hill and crossed the street at the light, then headed south down the long road, the gutters not yet cleared of the small gravel used to give icy streets traction in winter. A few blocks farther, she left the road on the left and went through some apartment buildings, where she came to the beginning of the beach path. Another kilometer along it and she would be at her favorite spot on the shore. As she walked along the narrow dirt walkway, long grasses brushing against her legs, her father's words repeated themselves like a pounding headache.

She hugged herself as if it would make up for all the hugs her father had never given her. The ocean was on her right, a wooded area on her left so thick the apartment buildings and homes beyond weren't visible. Annela could almost believe she was in the country, kilometers away from the bustle of Helsinki. She rounded the shore until she came to the large stone protrusion that, as a child, she had named "Elephant Rock." It looked like an elephant's head with wide ears and a short trunk winding toward the sea.

Annela walked onto the rock and sat just above the point where one of the elephant's eyes met the icy ocean. The wind tousled her hair and blew strands of it into her eyes. Although it was early April, winter had yet to give up its hold, and the ocean hadn't yet melted. Because of the ice there was no gentle lap of waves at her feet, and she knew it might be another month before she'd hear that again.

She wondered where she would be living next, whether she'd even be close enough to visit her Elephant Rock on any regular basis.

When she moved, she might not belong to the Marjaniemi Ward anymore, either. It had been a blessing to live only a ten-minute walk from the chapel, when so many others had to travel much farther. She lowered her head, and a single tear slipped down her cheek. Annela sniffed and wiped it away with disdain.

It wasn't as if this was the first time her father had turned her away. After a lifetime of insult and criticism, she should have been immune to her father's outbursts, she reasoned. Because of him, home had rarely been a place of comfort. But somehow his refusing to let her return to the only home she had ever known was worse. It pierced her deeper than she would have expected it to.

What made him react so harshly to her today? Was he upset over her change in faith? It wasn't as if her father were a particularly devout Lutheran. He rarely attended church. And he hadn't come to the Easter service in years, coming to last year's Christmas service only after weeks of her mother's pleading.

No, it wasn't that Annela was leaving their church. It was that she was joining the Mormons. The fact that Annela had given her parents' names to the missionaries as a referral likely didn't help matters. Her father had dismissed them with orders to never return.

Annela remembered her father's voice over the telephone when he told her about sending the missionaries away. "I know they're hand-some and American," he had said. "But that doesn't mean you have to fawn all over them and believe every word they say."

Annela smiled at the memory in spite of her watery eyes. Young men years her junior didn't appeal to her—their message did, however. Her father just didn't understand. Annela had known from the elders' first visit, when they spoke of Joseph Smith, that they spoke truth. At first she knew on a logical level. What they had taught made so much sense, answered so many of the questions her religion teachers in grade school had always brushed off.

"Why aren't there prophets anymore?" she had once asked.

"God doesn't work that way today," her teacher, Mr. Ahonen, had said. "Besides, we aren't supposed to wonder about such things." Her other teachers had given her variations on that response. Annela had almost given up asking questions when the missionaries came. The elders had hardly gotten any words out before she interrupted.

"Why aren't there prophets anymore?"

"Actually, there are," Elder Densley had said. He went on to explain the Apostasy and Restoration, and Annela found herself leaning forward as if she might miss a word if she didn't.

But that logical belief had turned into something much stronger. She had come to know in her heart that the missionaries' message was true, and the time to act on that knowledge had arrived. She couldn't put it off any longer, even if it meant leaving Tommi and postponing her master's degree studies, since she probably wouldn't have school money for at least a year now.

A pebble skittered across the rock and landed on the white sheet of ice below her feet. She looked over her shoulder to find the source, a man with blond hair and a dark blue coat approaching.

"Hey," he called. "I thought I'd find you here."

Tommi. Annela couldn't decide whether she was glad to see him. She should be, since she hadn't seen him for three weeks. And she usually welcomed his smile, especially at emotional times, but today was different. "How did you know I was here?"

"When I got home you weren't there. I called your cell phone. Then I tried your parents. Your mom said you had left ten minutes before. Since I could hear your dad booming in Swedish, I guessed that something had happened and you came here to escape." Annela's father was from Swedish stock, and that side came out during his tirades.

Tommi took a seat beside Annela and kissed her cheek. "It's good to be back. I've missed you."

"I've missed you too," Annela said. She leaned her head against his shoulder and looked across the frozen sea. It was a relief to know she didn't have to speak. She and Tommi felt no obligation to make small talk with each other. They gazed at the ocean inlet before them, encircled by land. There was only a small opening to the ocean. An island of rock and pine trees in the center blocked any view of the sea beyond.

"It's strange to think that this is really part of the ocean, isn't it?" Tommi said after a few minutes. "It looks like a lake, but it's part of the ocean, part of a greater whole." Annela nodded mechanically. Sometimes Tommi embarked on philosophical tangents, and while she often listened to them with interest, she didn't want to hear one now.

She had too much on her mind. She could still hear the echo of the apartment door slamming and the sound of her father's voice hollering in Swedish on the other side. Normally his outbursts embarrassed Annela unbearably. Most Finns never drew attention to themselves unless drunk. She too preferred to blend into the crowd—and succeeded except when Tommi's sheer lack of inhibition prevented it. Her father didn't require a drink to shed restraint like an old overcoat, although alcohol intensified his temper considerably.

Annela glanced at Tommi. His family was also from Swedish stock, and he must have inherited the accompanying temperament. Funny she hadn't. Part of her wished she had. It would make a lot of things easier to bear.

Tommi nudged her with his elbow. "So what's behind those tears?" Annela hadn't noticed that her cheeks were wet again. She made a swipe at them with the back of her hand, and Tommi patted her knee in reassurance. "Is your dad still upset that you're still seeing those 'American boys'?"

Annela nodded. "Yes, it's about the missionaries. But I wish you wouldn't call them that. It makes you sound like my dad."

"Oh, no. And we can't have that," Tommi said with an apologetic grin.

Tommi hadn't taken her investigation into the Church seriously, but then he hadn't been around to see most of it, either. Even so, such comments felt as if he were trying to undercut her. He removed his coat and put it around her shoulders, then reached for her hand.

"Maybe your dad just needs some time to cool off. Bringing up the missionaries and their book is probably not the best way to stay on his good side, you know. Just give him some space."

"It's not just the missionaries," Annela said with a shake of her head.

His eyebrows came together and he pulled back. "Then what is it?"

Annela licked her lips and paused before answering. "I've decided to get baptized."

Tommi let out the breath he had been holding. "Is that all? I thought maybe you really *were* going to dump me for one of the elders." He chuckled with a nervous edge to his voice.

Wondering how to explain what her decision meant without upsetting him too much, she looked away.

"Annela, " Tommi said, reaching for her. He turned her to face him. "What aren't you telling me?"

"I have to move out," Annela said bluntly.

Tommi's eyebrows furrowed. "But why? Things are going so well between us." He reached for her hands and held them between his own with a firm grip. "I know we haven't been living together that long, but I thought we were adjusting. What happened?"

"I decided to get baptized, that's what happened," Annela said, pulling her hands away. "I can't live with you anymore. Either I move out or we get married."

Tommi's jaw hardened. He looked away. "Oh, I see. You're trying to trap me into a commitment. I didn't see this coming. Let me guess, you're pregnant, too?" he said tonelessly.

Annela covered her face with her hands for a moment. "Tommi, you don't get it, do you? This is not about *us*. It's about—"

"It's about the missionaries. You *do* have it for one of them, don't you?"

"Tommi, please—" She hated this side of him, the unpredictable, moody one.

He cut her off. "I can't believe you'd let something so trivial like this come between us. I thought we had something really special. I thought there was a reason we found each other again after all those years. I was convinced it couldn't be a coincidence that my best friend from grade school just happened to come into the restaurant that day. What a fool I was."

He made a move to stand up, but Annela grabbed his arm and pulled him back down. "Please, Tommi. Listen for a minute. This is just as hard for me. But I know the elders' message is true. I know it. And now I have to do something about it." His face still looked blank, but she pressed on in hopes of finding some way to give him a glimmer of understanding. "It's as if—as if God let me see into His mind for just a moment, and now He expects me to act on that knowledge. If I don't, I'm running from Him. He has given me a gift, and I can't throw it back in His face." She searched Tommi's eyes for a sign of understanding, but found only hurt.

They sat in awkward silence for a moment until Tommi finally said, "So . . . when are you leaving?"

"As soon as I can. My father won't let me stay with them."

"So we aren't over?"

Annela smiled at him, grateful that he was coming around. "Of course not."

Tommi nodded. "Good." His arm slipped around her shoulders. He was only a few centimeters taller than Annela, so she had to slouch down to rest her head on his shoulder, but the closeness was reassuring. She closed her eyes. Tears came in earnest now, and she let them come. Tommi's embrace eased the loneliness, and she decided she was glad he had come. He held her close for some time without saying a word. She was grateful he didn't try to soothe her right now. He wouldn't have known the right thing to say and wouldn't have been able to say it with his heart if he did.

Annela's breath evened, and her eyes gradually dried. Tommi turned his head to look at her, sympathy on his face. She forced a smile. He wiped a tear from her cheek with his thumb.

"Your nose is red again."

She choked on a chuckle and covered her nose with both hands. Whenever she cried, it deepened to a dark red bordering on purple, swelled up three sizes, then stayed that way for hours. Tommi brushed a stray piece of hair from her face.

"I hate to see my girl hurting. It makes me miserable too."

She looked into his pale blue eyes and wished his words would ease the ache. He was trying so hard. Tommi leaned closer, and his lips parted ever so slightly. But instead of leaning in, Annela found herself pulling away, avoiding his kiss. She couldn't be romantic—not at a time like this.

Tommi pulled back, holding her out at arm's length. "What is it?"

"I'm sorry," she said helplessly, searching for an explanation, which he wouldn't understand, because *she* didn't even know why she shied away. She groped for an answer. "It's just that I am feeling so many emotions right now, and there is no space left to feel anything more." It was a lame explanation, she knew, but it would have to suffice.

Tommi released his hold on her shoulders. "I didn't think kissing was against your new religion," he said with a bite in his voice. He knew as well as she did that baptism had nothing to do with her pulling away, but the comment still hurt. He stood and brushed off his jeans.

"Tommi, don't go. I'm sorry."

He avoided looking at her. "I'll be at the apartment."

Annela nodded and watched him walk away across the Elephant Rock, wishing she could call and bring him back. Wishing he could understand.

CHAPTER 2

Alone once more, Annela pulled her knees to her chest and thought, this time about Tommi. If only he could understand what the gospel meant to her. Ever since that first discussion he had brushed off her interest in the Book of Mormon as a passing fancy. He hadn't been there for the initial discussion, so the first time he heard about it was when he had come home from work and she had rushed to him, eyes shining, Book of Mormon clutched in hand.

"Tommi, you have got to read this," she had said as he hastily tossed his shoes on the pile by the door. She pulled him to the couch and plopped onto it. "Come here. Look at this." She opened the book and began flipping pages.

Tommi's face had confusion written all over it as he sat down. "What is that?" he asked, pointing at the book.

She held it up so he could see the cover and articulated each word she read. "The Book of Mormon."

Tommi's eyebrows rose. "That American cult book? Since when were you interested in cults?"

"It's not a cult," Annela said, index finger now tracking columns of text. "The missionaries gave it to me. Read this. Right here." She tapped the page with her finger a few times. "This is where Lehi's dream starts, and here . . ." She flipped to a spot held by her other hand ". . . is where his son Nephi gets the interpretation from an angel."

Tommi said nothing, but indulged her. He leaned over and read along with her about the field, the rod of iron, and the river. "What's the point?" he asked, sincerely bewildered.

"We haven't gotten to that part yet," Annela said. "First, read about the tree." She read the rest of the dream aloud, then fell back against the couch and hugged the book. "Isn't that beautiful?"

Tommi's face looked blank. "I think I lost you somewhere around the spacious building."

"Nephi explains it here," she said, turning to Nephi's description. Annela read aloud about the tree of life, the love of God, the word of God, and the pride of the world. She finished and closed the book with a sigh. "Doesn't it just make you feel good inside?"

Tommi flashed a warm smile. "I sure do feel good. But I'm not sure whether it's the book or you sitting so close that's making me feel that way." He leaned over and placed a gentle kiss on her mouth. She opened her eyes and smiled. He kissed her again, then with one hand took the book from her and placed it behind him. Annela had been so enraptured by the book, and Tommi, for that matter, that she didn't realize the implication of what he had done.

Until now. Annela sat up straight, indignant. A flood of memories returned of all the times she had brought up the Book of Mormon, excited about a passage she had found: Nephi getting the brass plates, Abinadi's courage, or Christ blessing the children—her favorite part. But whenever she had tried to share any of it with Tommi, he had appeased her for the moment, closed the book, put it aside—and kissed her.

Annela felt sick. Every tender memory from the week before his trip was tainted. She could no longer tell which kisses had any real meaning and which were a convenient escape. No wonder she had shied away moments ago. No wonder her feelings for him were fading.

For the first time, Annela admitted to herself that the more Tommi discounted her feelings about the Church, the more her feelings for him had changed. It had happened so slowly she hadn't noticed at first, even that she really hadn't missed him while he was gone. And now his touch no longer sent flutters through her.

She shivered in the cold, feeling completely and utterly alone, the loneliness harsh and empty. It was different from the loneliness she had grown up with where she had the misfortune of being an unplanned surprise, something her father never failed to remind her about. Tommi had been the first person to tell Annela he loved her, something not even her mother had given her. Maybe that was why she had felt safe and happy with him.

Annela reached into her purse for a Geisha chocolate bar. She unwrapped it and put a square into her mouth, letting the nutty filling melt before chewing the chocolate and taking another square. She glanced at the package, remembering why she loved Geisha bars so much.

It had been Christmas morning when she was eight years old. Annela awoke to find a small package beside her pillow. Inside she found four Geisha bars and a box of French pastel mints. She didn't know where they had come from, but she had known enough to hide the loot and not mention it to anyone. Otherwise she knew she would have to share it with the whole family, leaving little for her.

Every Christmas morning after that, Annela found the same package. It became her personal treasure, and she treated it as such. Each day she allowed herself either five mints or a square of a Geisha bar. The treats always lasted into the new year.

When Kirsti grew older, Annela expected that her sister would start finding a matching package by her pillow, too, but she didn't. The thought crossed Annela's mind that maybe Kirsti was keeping hers a secret too, but then Kirsti never had been one to keep quiet about anything. She would have made sure Annela knew of the candy and would have taunted her with it. Kirsti wouldn't have been expected to share, either. That was just the way things were.

Annela continued to keep her secret and imagined fantastic reasons behind the candy. Dad really loved her best. Santa knew she was a good girl after all. A fairy left it. As she grew older, Annela decided it had been her mother's meager attempt to show her love.

She stretched her legs, realizing how stiff they had become in the cold, and decided it was time she returned to the apartment. She would sleep on the couch tonight and start looking for a place to stay in the morning. Instead of going down the beach trail, she took the shorter route by walking up the hill behind the beach to a road lined with houses and trees, with a large gray boulder on her right. Heading down a nearby bike path, she spotted a bus stop. Not five minutes later bus number 93 arrived to take her home. She found a window seat and rested her head against it. She stared out into the evening sky, which was still quite light, being less than two months before *Juhannus*, the longest day of the year, when even the night had no darkness.

Tommi would still be angry when she got home, that was certain. She wondered whether he would be in his sulky mood or his yelling one.

When she reached their apartment building and began climbing the stairs, dread began to build in her stomach like a heavy weight. She paused in front of their door for a moment, took a deep breath, then pushed the key into the lock and opened the door. A delicious aroma wafted across her and mood music played on the stereo.

"Tommi?" Annela said, closing the door and looking around. Her shoes clicked softly on the hardwood floor. She kicked them off and hung her purse on the hook behind the door, then stepped into the living room.

In the middle of the area rug Tommi had set up a card table set with Annela's best dishes and a freshly pressed white tablecloth. A single long-stemmed rose rested in a glass vase in the center. Tommi emerged from the kitchen, carrying two steaming plates of food and wearing a grin.

"Welcome back," he said. "I was hoping you'd get here soon." He leaned down and kissed her cheek, then placed the dishes on the table. Pulling out one chair, he motioned toward it and said, "M'lady."

Annela couldn't contain her smile. She sat on the chair and watched him walk around to the other side of the table and sit across from her. "This is quite a surprise," she said. "It's beautiful."

Tommi flashed one of his classic smiles and reached across the table for her hands. "I thought I'd get a jump start on making the most of our last night together, that's all."

"Then you're not upset?"

Tommi shook his head. "Of course not. You have to do what you have to do." He shook out his linen napkin and placed it in on his lap, then reached toward the floor beside him and produced a bottle of white wine.

"You know I can't drink that," Annela said.

Tommi reached for her glass. "You're not baptized yet," he reminded her as he poured the sparkling drink. "Consider it one last time."

He pushed the glass across the table. Annela pushed it right back.

Tommi set the bottle onto the table with a thud. "This is expensive stuff. I bought it just for you."

"I'm sorry, but I can't."

Tommi didn't answer. Instead he gulped down his wine and refilled his glass. He took his fork and pierced carrot medallions and new potatoes, then shoved them into his mouth. Annela reached for his hand. She needed to give him credit for trying. Still chewing, he looked up with a challenging glare.

"Thank you for tonight," Annela said. "It was such a wonderful surprise. Let's not ruin it by fighting, okay? I'll just get myself some water."

When she returned, Tommi wasn't sitting quite as stiffly. His herring and vegetables were half gone, but he was no longer attacking his food. Annela began eating her own meal.

"Remember my first day of school?" Tommi asked with a warmer look in his eyes. "Yours was the prettiest face in the room."

Annela nodded, smiling at the memory. She and Tommi were in fourth grade when he had moved into her school class. They had been best friends almost immediately.

"I don't think I ever told you what that year meant to me," she said. "It was the first and only time that I didn't feel alone in the world. It crushed me when you moved away the next summer."

"And all those years later you walked into my restaurant . . . and you were the prettiest face in the room." Tommi reached across the table and stroked her face. "Since that day I have been happier than ever before."

Annela blushed and looked down.

Tommi went on. "We've had some good times, haven't we? Remember the stilts?"

Annela laughed out loud. "How could I forget? But it wasn't just the stilts. You were also singing at the top of your lungs. You have always loved embarrassing me."

She remembered cringing at the feigned inattention of people as they walked past, pretending not to look but eyeing them out of the corner of their eyes anyway. As long as Tommi didn't drag her into the spotlight with him, she laughed along. That was last June, on *Juhannus*. Could midsummer night really have been less than a year ago? Everything before the missionaries seemed a lifetime ago to her.

As they spoke, other memories tumbled out. She remembered the countless hours she and Tommi had spent swimming at the beach during the summer and even the fall, freezing water notwithstanding. She remembered the first time they sat on Elephant Rock together and watched the sunset. And he had kissed her for the first time on the very spot where they had sat earlier that day.

"I've got lots of ideas for making memories before you leave," Tommi said, a light coming into his eye. He stood up, placed his napkin beside his plate and held out a hand for Annela. Knowingly, she stood up and settled into dance position. The two of them began to sway to the music, and Annela rested her head against his shoulder. Tommi stroked her hand with his thumb and leaned his head against hers, then turned to kiss her. This time Annela willingly kissed him back. Their dance gradually stopped as the kiss grew stronger. Tommi's hands released Annela's. He pulled her close, then slowly reached in front for the buttons on her blouse.

The spell broke. Annela pushed him back, her head shaking back and forth.

"No, Tommi." Her voice was laced with frustration. "You don't understand at all, do you?"

Tommi wiped some lipstick off his mouth with his thumb. "I thought I understood perfectly. Wasn't it your idea to have a final night together?"

Annela stepped farther back, her hand raised in protest. "This is not what I meant. I'm sorry if that's what you thought. But I can't."

It was as if a switch had flipped inside Tommi. The look in his eyes made Annela cringe. She could tell that one of his yelling moods was coming on. With a single swipe, Tommi knocked the table over, spilling everything onto the area rug and wood floor, and shattering the wine glasses. Annela's heart jumped in her chest as blood drained from her face.

"Get out," he bellowed, his arm extended, pointing to the door. "Get out of my sight!"

He had always had a temper, but this was worse than usual. She stepped forward, hoping to bring out the charming protector side of him. "Tommi—"

But he wouldn't listen. He grabbed her by both shoulders and pushed her to the door. "I said get out," he hissed into her face.

Annela stumbled into her shoes, grabbed her purse, and moments later stood in the corridor with the door slammed in her face. Her throat grew tight, and she fought a burning behind her eyes. She had never seen Tommi *this* angry. Every so often he had taken his anger out on things and broken them, but nothing of value. And once, when his hockey team lost, he hit the wall and left a fist-sized hole in it. But this was way beyond all that.

She headed for the bus stop, unsure where she would go. Home? She glanced at her watch. If her father followed his typical routine after one of his tirades, he would be out drinking right now. It might be safe to slip inside for the night.

Less than half an hour later she stood in front of the old apartment. After turning the key, she opened the door slowly to avoid creaking the old hinges. Stale cigar smoke wafted into the hall and Annela stopped cold. She held her breath and peered inside. She saw no one. Despite her relief, she took tiny steps all the way to the back bedroom before allowing herself to breathe easily. The other bedroom door opened, and her mother's face appeared.

"Annela?" she whispered. "Is that you?"

Annela nodded. Her mother tiptoed across the hall, and the two of them quickly closed the bedroom door behind them. "I need someplace to stay tonight," Annela said under her breath.

Her mother glanced toward the door and back again. Annela noticed swelling in her mother's left eye. Her father's handiwork, no doubt. "You can stay. But let's keep it a secret."

"Of course," Annela said. "I won't come out in the morning until you call me."

Her mother gave a knowing and relieved smile. "Thanks."

Kirsti sat up in bed. "What's going on?"

Their mother put a finger to her lips. "Shhh. Annela is staying here tonight. Don't let Dad know. Okay?"

Annela held her breath. She wouldn't put it past Kirsti to get her into trouble, but this time her mother would pay too, if their father found out. Kirsti mumbled something in her sleep and rolled over.

She and her mother each sighed in relief. They set up a makeshift blanket bed on the floor, and soon Annela was lying down, trying to sleep. She didn't know how long she lay there. She felt hollow inside.

Now what? She would have to drop out of school. She had no job, no place to stay, and no one to turn to. Not one real friend.

She had thought that living in a home with no love had hardened her against loneliness. Having Tommi in her life to care for her and watch over her had partially filled that void. But now she knew she'd be learning what true loneliness was.

CHAPTER 3

Helena didn't sleep well that night. She kept listening for her husband to come in, worrying that he would discover Annela in the other bedroom. Around seven o'clock the next morning, she got out of bed. Oskar hadn't returned. She hoped he was all right. He had never been hurt on his nights out, but she still worried. Then again, when he was drunk, it was easier when he left the house. She was grateful he hadn't come back yet. It might give her a chance to talk to Annela before she left.

A knock sounded on the apartment door, and Helena started with surprise. Did Oskar forget his key? She put on her robe, then shut the girls' bedroom door as she passed it. Peering through the peephole, she recognized Tommi. She breathed a sigh of relief and opened the door.

"Good morning, Mrs. Sveiberg," Tommi said. "Is Annela here?"

Helena ran her fingers through her bed-flattened hair and glanced over her shoulder. "Yes, but she's still asleep. Is everything all right between you two? She seemed pretty upset last night." She looked over Tommi's shoulder, afraid Oskar would show up.

Tommi shrugged. "I said some things I shouldn't have. That's why I brought these." He held out the looped carrying string at the top of a package of flowers. "Would you give them to her? With this?" He held out a card in the other hand.

"Of course," Helena said, taking both items. "Would you . . . like to come in?"

Tommi shook his head. "No, but thank you. I need to get to the restaurant."

Helena closed the door and headed to the kitchen. She laid the flowers and card on the counter, then put a kettle of water on the stove for some chamomile tea. After she'd learned about the Word of Wisdom from Annela, she had stopped drinking coffee and switched to herbal teas. Of course, she made sure Oskar didn't know that.

Helena eyed the clock, wondering how much longer it would be until he returned. Probably not for another hour, judging by the other times he had gone drinking all night. She went back to her bedroom, where she opened a drawer in her nightstand and withdrew several books. She flipped through the pages, pulling out bills that she had hidden between the pages—a ten-mark bill here, a twenty there, even one fifty-mark and two hundred-mark bills. Not that much individually, but after collecting her stash from half a dozen different books that served as hiding places, she had a tidy sum. The money should help Annela get started in a place of her own, she thought.

She folded the wad in half and put it in the pocket of her robe before replacing the books where they belonged. Then she went across the hall to the other bedroom and knocked. The door creaked as she pushed it open. Helena poked her head into the room. She whispered so as to not wake Kirsti.

"Annela, are you awake?"

Annela opened her eyes and pushed up onto one elbow. "I am now. Do you need something?" She pushed her hair away from her face and rubbed her eyes. She grimaced.

Helena entered and leaned over. "Are you feeling sick?"

"I've got a headache, but I'm fine," Annela said, forcing a smile. "I just realized that my eyes are swollen. My nose is probably all red, too, isn't it?"

"That happened even as a girl when you cried at night," her mother said with a wistful smile. "Are you all right?"

"I'll be fine," Annela said with a nod.

"You look beautiful."

Annela chuckled. "Thanks, Mom. But I know better."

Helena glanced at Kirsti, who still slept deeply. "Come here. I want to talk to you."

"Is Dad home?"

Helena shook her head. "Not yet. That's why I wanted to talk to you now, while we've got the chance."

Annela stood and followed her out of the room. The tea kettle was whistling, so Helena went to the kitchen and prepared two mugs of tea. Annela sat at the tiny table, and Helena set one of the mugs of tea in front of her. She joined Annela at the table and clasped her hands around the mug, trying to steady as well as warm them.

She spoke in a whisper. "I am sorry about last night, Annela. Your father just has a temper, and when he doesn't understand something, he figures it must be bad. He does have a good heart, deep down."

Annela glanced at the spot on Helena's face that had swollen and started to change colors. "But he hit you again."

Helena smiled. "He has problems. We all do. But he has always been a good provider, and he'll always be faithful to me. And in spite of it all . . . I do love him."

"It's my fault he hit you this time. I'm sorry, Mom."

Helena patted Annela's knee and smiled weakly. "Don't you worry yourself about me. I can handle it."

Annela sniffed. "What he does to you is horrible. You shouldn't put up with it."

Helena bit her lip and willed away a multitude of thoughts and memories. "It's more complicated than that," she finally said. "The truth is, I should have walked out the door the first time he hit me. Actually, I did leave once." Her voice had grown quiet as she thought of the day she'd walked out, how her parents didn't believe that Oskar could do such a thing, how . . . She shook her head to clear her mind. This wasn't the time to think about those times.

"Why did you come back?" Annela asked.

Helena gave her daughter a wan smile. "Because he showered me with gifts and apologies and promises to never do it again, and because I believed him. I think he believed himself."

"And why did you stay when he kept hitting you?"

For a moment Helena wanted to tell the entire to story to Annela, but she couldn't. Maybe another time. She looked down and closed her eyes. "I owed it to him," she said in almost a whisper. She patted Annela's hand. Her daughter looked confused. "It's a long story. But trust me. I have my reasons."

"Such as?"

Helena waved her hand. "It doesn't matter. Remember, your father and I have a long history that goes back well before you were born. Even if we didn't, well . . . It's a bit late to try to walk out the door now, isn't it?" She took a deep breath, then reached for the honey pot. Her hands suddenly busy with scooping honey and stirring it into her tea, Helena continued, "Anyway, I just wanted to let you know that I don't mind your getting baptized, even if Dad does. And maybe . . . maybe someday I can join you."

Annela's eyes shot fully open. "What?"

Helena grinned. "I didn't want the missionaries to leave. It was your father who sent them away."

Annela suddenly seemed tongue-tied. "I had no—no idea," she stammered.

"And neither does he," Helena said. "Let's keep it that way for now. But I want you to be baptized, and I want to be there." She reached into the pocket of her robe and pulled out the money. "I've been saving a little here and there. Didn't really know why until now. I want you to have it. It's not a lot, but it should cover at least one month's rent to get you started."

She placed the bills in Annela's hand, then held onto it. Annela looked from the money to her mother and back again. "I can't take this."

"Yes, you can," Helena said, wanting to tell her daughter how much she loved her, how proud she was of her. But as with so many things, it was a little late to start that now.

"Oh, there's one more thing," Helena said, standing up and going to the counter. She returned with the flowers and held out the string for Annela to take. "Tommi brought this by. He didn't want to come in. Just left them and this card for you."

Annela took the flowers and the card as Helena sat down again. "He seemed worried. Are things all right between you two?"

Annela shrugged and began opening the floral wrapping. "I don't know."

Inside lay three white roses nestled in baby's breath. Annela tore open the envelope and read the card.

She read the note, then looked up and grinned. "Tommi wants to learn about the Church. He says he's sorry and doesn't want religion to come between us. And he started reading the Book of Mormon last night."

Helena smiled. "Even if it's for your sake, it's a start."

Annela nodded, excitement in her eyes. "And if he gets baptized, then maybe—" But she stopped before finishing the thought and shrugged instead. "Ever since I learned about eternal families, it's been a dream for me to have a temple marriage, and now maybe, just maybe someday Tommi and I can . . ."

"I hope so. For your sake," Helena said, but her heart wasn't in it. Annela seemed to notice her hesitation.

"You don't think he'll believe?"

"It's not that," Helena said, stirring her tea absently. Annela waited for her to continue, so she set the spoon aside and went on. "It's just that Tommi reminds me a lot of your father at that age. I worry about you, what he might do to you."

Annela looked away. Her eyes got shiny, but she didn't say anything. Helena knew she had hit close to a nerve. She wondered if Tommi had struck Annela, whether this conversation was connected to what had happened last night.

Annela glanced at the kitchen clock. "I'd better go if I want to get to church on time."

"Of course," Helena said.

* * *

Annela returned to the apartment, hoping Tommi had already left for work. She didn't want anything to mar her good mood. Besides, she wasn't sure what to make of Tommi's flowers and card. She needed more time to think over their relationship and what, if anything, she should do about it. When she saw that Tommi's shoes weren't by the door and his jacket was gone, she nodded in relief. She wouldn't have to face him quite yet.

As she set her purse on the end table by the door, she thought of the money inside and smiled. Her mother really did care about her, and not just Kirsti. And someday maybe her mother would be able to join her in the Church.

An hour later Annela entered the Marjaniemi Ward building and scanned the long hall for Elder Densley and Elder Stevens. The latter had been transferred to Helsinki just two weeks before, but Elder Densley was the one who first taught Annela and had been working with her toward baptism ever since. She knew the elders were hoping that she would make the commitment before Elder Densley left for home.

As she scanned the foyer and hallway, she didn't see the missionaries right off, so she tried the chapel itself, but didn't see them in there, either. She found a seat on one of the side pews, and shortly the meeting began. She watched the sacrament pass by with yearning. Granted, she could partake if she wanted to—but it wouldn't mean anything, not really, until she was baptized, so she had decided to wait. It wouldn't be long now, she thought. Soon she too would be able to partake of the bread and water and renew her baptismal covenants. *Her* baptismal covenants! The thought sent a warm thrill through her.

When sacrament meeting ended Annela stood to scan the room for the elders. She found them sitting on the bench by the door. Perhaps they had arrived late. She didn't quite reach them before the typical throng of girls swarmed around them, vying for the attention of the American men. Two Laurels arrived before she did, coyly batting their lashes. Annela hoped she could still catch the elders and share her news with them. Elder Densley noticed her and grinned, looking grateful for a way to gracefully extricate himself from the conversation.

"Annela!" he called out. Then, to the young women, "You'll have to excuse me. I need to speak with our investigator for a moment."

Elder Densley stepped to one side, allowing her room to approach. He smiled in response to her grin and held out his hand.

"Tommi came home yesterday," Annela said. "And I told him."

"What did he say?" Elder Densley asked.

"He was pretty upset. But he hasn't changed my mind. I spent last night at my parents' place, and I'm moving out today."

"Really? I mean, that's great!" Elder Densley said. "So that means you'll be staying with your parents now?"

"Um, no. I don't have anyplace to go. But I think last night was my biggest test, and I passed."

"Tommi called us last night and we set up an appointment with him on Tuesday," Elder Densley said, consulting his appointment book. "I thought maybe he was planning to get baptized too, and then the two of you would get baptized together."

"No, not that, either. I didn't know he had called you already." A glimmer of hope sparked inside her. She bit her lips together. If Tommi found the gospel, things could change. They would be able to share so much more than literature and music and intellectual dinner conversation as they had for years. And they would be closer than they had been lately—like old times, before his angry moods had gotten bad. Butterflies awakened inside, and she felt giddy at the thought.

"So what are you going to do?" Elder Densley asked.

"Well, I still need to find a place to live, but I'm moving out today, regardless. I've got a little money, so I'll be living in a hotel until I can find an apartment. But I'm getting baptized, and that's all there is to it."

Elder Densley gave Annela a high five, the closest he could get to a hug within mission rules. "All right!"

Elder Stevens came over and grinned. "You look happy today," he said to Annela. "I take it your parents will let you stay with them?"

Annela shook her head. "Nope. In fact, my father says I'll be dead to him as soon as I join the Church." She shrugged. "I figure if I take a leap of faith, the Lord will provide a net for me to land on, right?"

"Let's get that net under you as fast as we can then," Elder Stevens said, pulling out his appointment book. "Let's set an official date. The sooner you leap, the sooner the Lord will provide, right? How about Saturday?"

Annela's face split into a grin. "That would be great." She felt an arm go about her waist and looked over to see Sister Henderson, one of the elderly *mummos* of the ward. She had taken Annela under her wing since finding her crying in the church rest room one Sunday after a fight with Tommi.

Sister Henderson hadn't ignored Annela's tears, although it had actually embarrassed Annela at the time. She didn't know Sister Henderson, and the woman certainly didn't know her, either.

Annela had been sitting on a chair against the rest room wall. Sister Henderson crouched down to look at her, even though she was so short she didn't need to. "Something is terribly wrong if such a beauty is crying," she had said. Annela appreciated the effort to cheer her up by playing on her vanity, but it didn't help. She knew too well how she looked when she cried.

When Annela didn't respond, Sister Henderson said, "What can I do?" She sat on the chair next to Annela's, fished in her purse for something, then pulled out a Geisha bar. When she waved it, Annela crumbled. Had it been anything else, she could have resisted, but not a Geisha bar.

"That's a start," Sister Henderson said with a contented nod. "I say chocolate is almost always the first step to feeling better." She leaned close and whispered, "Just between us, I'm glad chocolate isn't listed in the Word of Wisdom. We'd have a real problem if it were." She chuckled, her shoulders bouncing. Annela took a bite and smiled weakly as she dried her cheeks with a tissue.

"Much better," Sister Henderson said, patting Annela's knee.

As Annela ate the chocolate, Sister Henderson chatted. Not about anything in particular, but she didn't stop until the hall buzzed with conversation, signaling the end of Sunday School classes. Sister Henderson had managed to make Annela forget why she'd found refuge in the rest room in the first place, and had replaced the young woman's tears of sadness with those of genuine laughter.

Sister Henderson stood up. "It's time for Relief Society. Care to join me and watch all those old ladies fall asleep?" A burst of laughter escaped Annela. Not only was Sister Henderson not exaggerating, but Annela had to smile at the idea of her new elderly friend not considering herself an old lady.

After that week Sister Henderson fussed and worried over Annela, and while Tommi was gone, she invited Annela to dinner and insisted on hearing the latest news about him. So it was a familiar and endearing moment when Sister Henderson's arm slipped around Annela's waist as she spoke with the missionaries.

"What's this I hear about you moving?" she asked. "You aren't leaving the ward, are you? Don't you dare. I won't sit back and let myself lose a friend that easily, you know." One of her chubby fingers poked Annela for emphasis.

Annela laughed, reaching an arm around Sister Henderson's shoulders. "I hope not. I have to find a new place to live if I plan to get baptized on Saturday. And I can't stay in a hotel forever. But I hope to find something in the ward boundaries."

"Oh, good," Sister Henderson said, squeezing her waist with a motherly air. "I mean, it's not good that you have to move, but finding a place to stay within the ward is no problem."

Annela shook her head doubtfully. "I don't know. I hear decent, empty apartments are hard to find right now, especially in this part of the city."

Sister Henderson's index finger flew up and began wagging at Annela. "Now I won't have you saying my little apartment isn't fit to live in," she said with a sparkle in her eye. "And I won't have you saying no."

"Are you inviting me—"

"Nothing of the sort. I'm *telling* you you're going to live with me until you find some other place or get sick of me. No living in a hotel. That's ridiculous."

Annela put her arms around the sister's round form and gave her a hug. "Thank you, Sister Henderson. Elders, I think I found my net."

CHAPTER 4

After church, Annela went back to the apartment with plans to pack. She arrived still excited at the idea of being baptized so soon. She would have to find some boxes before she would be able to pack all her things, but for now she did a cursory job of going through her belongings, stacking them all in one area.

When she came to the bookcase, she paused. Several shelves were filled with books—novels, biographies, histories, science books, all kinds of literature. She traced her finger along the spines, remembering how she and Tommi had read each book together and discussed it afterward, sometimes late into the night. The top shelf had CDs they had bought together, including some from concerts they had attended. How could she decide which were hers and which belonged to Tommi? She finally decided to leave them all—and hope that some day the same titles would be lined up in her home again, after Tommi joined the Church.

With a shrug, she set to packing a toiletry bag and suitcase with several days' worth of clothes, knowing it would be some time before she could return to move out completely.

As she headed for the door, she realized that Tommi needed to know her plans. Otherwise he would assume she had left him and their relationship behind when he saw that her things were gone. She sat down to write a note, asking him to meet her at Elephant Rock, where she planned to explain it all, then reconsidered. She scratched it out. A note was too impersonal, she decided. She dialed his work number on the phone instead. A voice she didn't recognize answered and said Tommi wasn't available, so she left a message for him to meet at the

Rock at six o'clock that evening. Then she picked up her bags and headed for the bus stop to take her to Sister Henderson's apartment.

When Annela arrived, Sister Henderson opened the apartment door and ushered her inside. "Welcome," she said. "I made some fresh bread for the occasion, but first let's get you settled."

She led Annela into the small bedroom immediately off the front entryway. "We've got only one bedroom and it's yours."

Annela stepped back. "I can't take your only bedroom."

Sister Henderson turned around, fist on her hip. "Yes you can, and you will."

"But where will you sleep?"

Sister Henderson took a few steps down the tiny hall and pointed into the room at the end. "In there. I'll stay on the couch tonight. Now don't look so horrified. I've arranged to borrow a bed from a neighbor whose son just left for college, so I'll be nice and comfortable in there."

"But—"

Sister Henderson wouldn't hear any protestations. "I'm a determined old lady. You won't win this argument." She tilted her head and patted Annela's arm. "Besides, I don't need the luxury of privacy that a young woman does."

* * *

Tommi stood on Elephant Rock and stared out at the sea as he waited for Annela, the wind ruffling his hair. He thought back to the night before, then to this morning's roses and the words on his card. He breathed out heavily, hoping Annela had forgiven him.

She was right. He didn't understand. But that didn't mean he didn't really love her and want to be with her. The fact that he felt threatened by her decision to move out and join the Mormons proved that he loved her, right? His life had suddenly swirled out of control, and to say it felt uncomfortable was an understatement.

So he had decided to grasp the reins and pull things back into line. In two days he would be meeting with the missionaries. He hoped that Annela would see that he was trying to understand.

Not to believe and join, but to understand. He really wanted to understand.

Then again, if Annela just assumed he had begun to believe, that wouldn't hurt either, would it? He decided it would give them more to share.

Tommi suddenly smelled Annela's perfume and felt her arms wrap around him. She reached around and planted a kiss on his cheek. He turned about and broke into a grin when he saw her own wide smile.

"It's good to see you too," he said, putting his arms around her waist. He hugged her tightly. It was a relief to see her.

He decided not to kiss her just in case; he didn't want her to pull back again. *I'll give her a bit more time,* he told himself. *She'll come back. She knows I've got a temper, but she also knows I love her more than life itself.* The two of them began to stroll back to the shore and along the pathway leading through the trees. The spring breeze seemed almost warm as the sun filtered through treetops and made dancing patterns on the ground. Tommi put an arm around her shoulders and pulled her close.

"I didn't expect you to be in such a good mood," he said.

Annela shrugged and looked around her. "Everything just looks better today." She folded her arms and breathed in the spring air deeply. "For one thing, I'm a sucker for a pretty flower arrangement, and you know it. Trying to play with my heart, are we?" She gave his chest a light punch with her fist.

Tommi played innocent. "What? I thought they were pretty."

Annela jabbed him with her elbow. Tommi let out a melodramatic gasp and held his side, then hobbled over to a boulder off the path and writhed in mock pain. Annela joined him on the rock.

"And," she said, ignoring his theatrics and sitting beside him, "I found out from a reliable source that you've already got an appointment to start taking the discussions. You don't know what that means to me."

Tommi dropped his martyr's act and got a more serious tone to his voice. "You said yourself that this is the one thing we haven't really understood about each other, right? Nothing else has really come between us since the fourth grade."

Annela's eyes clouded momentarily. "Things have sometimes."

Tommi shook his head. "Not in this way. And that stuff doesn't really count. It's just my temper. But you know even those things were only because I love you. Listen. I figure your church makes you happy, so maybe it could do something for me, too."

The concern in Annela's eyes was replaced with a shake of her head and a smile. Her eyes lit up. "If you only knew how I've dreamed of hearing those words from you. Just wait until the Spirit whispers to you, too. You won't believe the change it will make in your life."

Tommi took Annela's hand and put his other hand on top of it gingerly. "If you only knew how much you've already changed my life." For the first time since he closed the door on her, he felt back in control. She seemed ready to take him back, and he uttered a silent thanks that the flowers had worked.

He leaned in and gave her a kiss, much softer and more mean-ingful than the one he had given her the night before when a very different kind of passion had come over him. When he pulled back, Annela rested her head on his shoulder, and the two sat in warm silence for a few moments.

"Oh! I almost forgot to tell you," Annela said, sitting up straight and almost knocking Tommi off the boulder.

He laughed as he regained his balance. "What is it?"

"I'm getting baptized on Saturday."

"Really? That's so soon." He knew his voice didn't sound as excited as it should. He tried harder. "Wow. That's great."

Annela's eyebrows came together. "You seem disappointed."

"No, I'm not," he said, brushing away her concern. "It's just that I thought it'd be neat if we could be baptized together. If I decide to get baptized, that is."

"Oh, Tommi, that is such a sweet thought. But . . . I can't wait."

Annela kissed Tommi's cheek. He sighed heavily and hoped that her pause didn't mean she'd suspected that he'd wanted to postpone her baptism.

* * *

Annela kept busy over the next week as she waited for her baptismal day to arrive, but the time still dragged. She and Tommi spent hours packing her things and taking them to Sister Henderson's place. They ate lunch together on the floor amid boxes and reminisced about their past.

"Do you really have to go?" Tommi asked again. "We haven't been this close for a long time, and now you're leaving."

"You know I can't stay," she said. "I wish I could. But thank you so much for the help."

She didn't go to Elephant Rock until the night before her baptism, when she went by herself, late. Sister Henderson lived much closer to the Rock than Tommi. But somehow Annela had sensed that her life was changing and that she wouldn't be going there as often. She felt alone and wished she could share the moment with someone who understood.

Not Tommi. He didn't understand. Not yet, at least. Sister Henderson didn't, either. As wonderful as she was, Sister Henderson couldn't understand what Annela was feeling tonight. She was about to step away from her family for good. Annela sat on the cold surface of the rock in the yellow-gray light of dusk and rested her chin on her knees.

The following morning she would be baptized. She would enter the warm water and finally join the one true Church. Annela thought back to when she'd called her mother a few minutes before she came to the beach.

"I'm coming to the baptism," her mother had said.

"I want you there, but I don't want Dad to hurt you again," Annela had protested. She didn't need to explain what that meant. But Helena would hear none of it.

"I'm coming," she said with finality. Annela didn't ask what excuse her mother would invent for her husband's benefit, since he wouldn't let her go otherwise—perhaps a dentist appointment?

Annela had paused on the other end of the line, a knot in her throat. "Thanks, Mom," she said. "I really do want you there. I just worry."

"I know."

Annela would have to permanently say good-bye to her mother after her baptism. She pressed her forehead into her knees and again wished the ocean had melted enough for her to hear the sound of waves lapping at her feet. If her father kept his threat and really considered her dead, the chances of seeing any of her family again were remote. Annela also feared for her mother. What would become of her when she returned from the baptism? Annela prayed she wouldn't be the cause of another bruise on her mother's face.

Annela clutched her Book of Mormon to her chest. She thought through one of her favorite passages, of Alma's prayer in the face of heavy persecution. He had asked simply to have his sorrow swallowed up in the joy of Christ, despite the oppression and wickedness around him. He did not ask for the persecution removed, she remembered. Just to be able to endure it with joy. And his prayer was answered.

That's what Annela needed right then; the joy of Christ to swallow up any feelings of despair—and anger—that her father's shadow might cast across her baptism.

* * *

The following morning Sister Henderson fussed over Annela as if she were a bride, curling Annela's desperately straight hair and even adding a little blush and lipstick, which, like so many other sisters, Sister Henderson never wore herself.

"I'm just going to ruin it all when I go under the water," Annela said in half-hearted protest.

"Yes, but you'll be a beauty before that," Sister Henderson said as she put another spray of something in Annela's hair.

The service was held in the large classroom used for the Primary. The folding curtain was pulled back, even though there weren't enough people there to fill both sides of the room. Chairs stood in even rows facing the baptismal font along the back wall. Only a few people attended, including Tommi and Helena, who both sat on the back row. Sister Henderson, who sat near the front, seemed about to burst with excitement. Elder Stevens gave a talk, and then it was time.

Annela went into the women's rest room to access the font, then closed her eyes to calm the trembling in her stomach. She stepped into the warm water and walked to Elder Densley, who came from the other side. When he took her hands, she found them shaking, not from cold, but from nervousness, anticipation, the Spirit—a whole host of things flooding through her. He raised his arm and spoke the words slowly and clearly, and then Annela felt him lower her body below the water and back up again. She could almost feel the old shell of another life fall away into the water behind her, and a joy she had not known filled her from head to toe.

On impulse, Annela threw her arms around Elder Densley in a hug. He took a stunned step back, and Annela sheepishly pulled away and held out her hand for a handshake. She hadn't meant to violate the mission rule in her excitement. Under any other circumstances, she would have been mortified, but right then it didn't matter. She was baptized, and God now saw her as one of His own. No one could take that from her.

Afterward, the small group of guests came to congratulate Annela—the bishop, Relief Society president, and three other sisters Annela had become friends with. Tommi waited in back as the Relief Society president chatted with Helena and the bishop discussed an investigator with the elders. Shifting his weight from side to side, Tommi alternately shoved his hands in his pockets, then pulled them out to run them through his hair. Annela greeted him with a hug.

"Thanks for coming," she whispered.

Tommi returned her hug. "Anything for my girl," he said before confirming their dinner date and heading out.

The elders hung around to talk with Annela until Elder Densley noticed Helena sitting in the back of the room. He nudged Elder Stevens, who wished Annela well before ducking out to leave mother and daughter alone. Elder Densley shut the door behind them with a soft click. Annela turned to her mother, who held a crumpled handkerchief in her hands. Her eyes were red, but she was smiling.

"Thank you for coming," Annela said. "I hope you don't get in trouble for it."

Helena changed the subject. "I'm proud of you, Annela. You are so beautiful today."

Annela laughed and made a comment about her straggling wet hair, then paused and added, "I'm so glad you came."

"Me too."

The two of them stood in silence for a few moments, neither willing to say the inevitable good-byes.

"Well, I need to go, I suppose," Helena said, glancing at her watch. "Your father is expecting me back in about twenty minutes."

"Yes, you better."

But neither made a motion to leave for another minute. "Oh, I almost forgot," Helena finally said, looking in her purse. She pulled out a pink envelope and handed it to Annela. "I couldn't find a greeting card that really worked for a Mormon baptism," she said with a smile. "But it's something, anyway."

"Thank you," Annela said, clutching the card.

Her mother made a move for the door handle, then turned around. "I'll try to keep in touch," she said. "As much as . . . as much as I can."

Annela nodded, understanding what she meant. She watched her mother walk away and close the door behind her. For a moment, Annela had the urge to run into the hall and stop her from going back to the apartment, where she knew her father would be waiting. He might be drunk or suspicious, and ready to hurt her. But she stopped herself, knowing that her mother wouldn't stay, and that any delay would mean a greater chance of another bruise.

Sinking to a folding chair, Annela opened the envelope. Inside she found a congratulatory card and five twenty-mark bills. It wasn't a huge sum, but Annela could imagine the sacrifices that her mother must have made to save it since her last gift at breakfast only a week ago. She probably went without her favorite cheese, walked instead of taking the bus, skipped a haircut—anything to save money in ways her husband wouldn't notice. Annela decided she would use the money to help pay Sister Henderson for food.

Annela read the words written at the bottom of the card, and her eyes suddenly filled with tears.

"Love, Mom," was all it said.

CHAPTER 5

Annela attended Tommi's discussions, making sure he understood each principle before the elders went on. It was three weeks since her baptism, only days since her confirmation, and Annela had yet to come off her spiritual high. The only thing missing was her mother. Annela prayed for her mother and found herself worrying about Kirsti, too, wondering how they were doing. But even with those concerns, Annela glowed. Tommi kept asking if she had done something new to her hair or had bought a new shade of lipstick.

"No," Annela answered each time. "I got baptized." Tommi would chuckle, as if that could hardly be the reason for her looking different. She hoped that he would soon understand and gain a testimony of his own, that his eyes would sparkle with the Spirit as well. She longed to read the scriptures with him, to share spiritual thoughts, to do all those things they could do only when he embraced the gospel. Sometimes she wished she could still be living with him. She missed curling up on the couch and watching old movies together. If she were there now, they could be discussing gospel questions together.

But Annela tried to be patient when, after three discussions, Tommi didn't seem any closer to making a commitment.

"Remember," Elder Densley reminded Annela when she told him her hopes. "It took *years* for Brigham Young to know, but once he did, there was no moving him from his commitment. I think that's how the Finnish people are. It takes a whole lot to get them into the water, but once they're baptized, they stay faithful to the end."

At the next discussion, Annela sat on the sofa beside Tommi, with the missionaries on chairs across from them. She begged the

Lord for it not to take quite so long with Tommi as it had with
Brigham Young, then felt guilty as soon as she'd made the request.
She had no right to ask the Lord to change His timetable. If it took
months—or years—then that's what it would have to be, she
reminded herself. And Elder Densley's "faithful to the end" sounded
worth waiting for.

Tommi listened carefully to the discussion, which pleased
Annela. He promised to keep reading the Book of Mormon and pray
about it, and the elders made their appointment for the following
Tuesday. Annela had felt the Spirit in the room, and hoped Tommi
had felt it too.

After the elders left, Tommi closed the door behind them and
turned back to Annela. She waited, butterflies flitting in her middle,
hoping for more than what he had said after the other discussions. He
placed the Book of Mormon on an end table and traced the gold
letters with one finger. He looked up at her. When he didn't say
anything, Annela took a step closer.

"What are you thinking?" she asked, trying to sound supportive
instead of overeager.

A gentle smile began to curl his lips before he answered. "It is a
fine message, isn't it?"

"Yes it is," Annela said. She waited for Tommi to go on, and when
he didn't said, "And?"

"And . . . I'm just starting out, Annela. Give me time."

Annela took two long strides to reach him and grasped his hand.
"But you felt that peaceful feeling, didn't you? That's the Spirit, as
Elder Densley said."

Tommi simply smiled and kissed her forehead. "I always feel good
around you, Annela. How will I ever know whether it's you or the
Spirit?"

Annela couldn't tell if he was serious or trying to make her feel
good, but she decided it didn't really matter. His next discussion was
in a week. And if he needed it, he could keep having them every
week. In time he would be ready to say yes to the challenge. After all,
he had promised to read the Book of Mormon and pray about it.

* * *

Annela's watch read a few minutes after five when she returned to Sister Henderson's building and climbed the stairs. She hated the corridors of apartment buildings; their hollow echoes and cold walls always made her want to hurry just to escape them. But she never took elevators, even if they were faster. They felt too confining, and their noises were disconcerting.

She opened the apartment door to the smell of ham and boiling new potatoes. Annela breathed in deeply. She left her shoes by the door and hung her jacket on a hook, then noticed another smell—cologne. Curious, she glanced down and found a pair of men's shoes on the floor. She took a step to her right down the entryway and peeked into the living room. A tall young man with dark hair sat on the couch. He spoke to Sister Henderson, who sat knitting in her rocking chair but stopped and looked toward the door when she heard the creak of Annela's step on the wood floor.

"Annela, you're home. Come in."

Annela entered the room and smiled, raising her eyebrows—unable to hide her curiosity about the visitor. Sister Henderson laid her knitting aside, then stood, her eyes twinkling a little more than usual, and gestured toward the man.

"This is Mika Lehto from the Haaga Ward. His grandmother and I have been friends since I joined the Church some thirty years ago."

Mika stood and put out his hand. "Nice to meet you," he said with a wide smile.

Annela couldn't help but notice his long lashes, which were dark and curled away from his brown eyes. He was tall. Surely he had to duck under doorways, she thought in amusement. He wore a navy blue Norwegian sweater that set off his dark coloring handsomely.

"Mika just returned from his mission to Norway," Sister Henderson said.

Annela smiled warmly as she shook his hand.

"He'll be staying for dinner," Sister Henderson went on, seeming rather pleased with herself.

"Sister Henderson will feed you well," Annela said.

"So I've heard," Mika replied with a wink. "The legendary stories of her dinners have reached Haaga as well."

"I'll just leave you two here to get acquainted while I finish making dinner," Sister Henderson said, trotting to the door and disappearing through it. Annela and Mika stood awkwardly in the middle of the room, and Annela panicked. She'd never been very good at keeping up polite conversation with strangers, and having a painfully good-looking man in front of her at the same time would only make things worse.

Annela inched toward the door. "I, uh, better see if she needs my help," she said. "I'll be right back."

Mika smiled with a nod, then sat on the couch again. When Annela reached the door she whirled around and raced to the kitchen.

Sister Henderson glanced from a steaming pot and shooed Annela away. "Get back out there."

"Let me help you with something," Annela begged, taking two hot pads from the counter and attempting to drain the pot of potatoes.

Sister Henderson slapped her hand lightly and took the pot from her. "You'll do no such thing," she said, replacing the potatoes on the stove. She put one hand on her hip and wagged her finger at Annela. "Now you get back out there and get to know that marvelous young man."

Annela stared at her in disbelief for a few seconds. "You mean you invited him for *my* benefit?" She looked over her shoulder as if she could see Mika through the walls. "You want the two of us to . . . you've got to be kidding. He's younger than I am." Young men in Finland had to complete military service before serving missions, so Mika was probably around twenty-three, only a year younger than Annela, but it was her best defense for the moment.

"Go, go, go," Sister Henderson said, this time bodily pushing her out of the kitchen. "He's a real catch. One of the few eligible LDS men in Helsinki, if you don't count the widowers. And he's handsome, too."

Annela stood in the hallway for just a moment, stunned at this new matchmaking career her friend had taken on. She took a deep breath and returned to their guest, determined to make small talk until Sister Henderson deemed they had had enough time alone and agreed to serve dinner.

"It'll be just a few minutes," Annela said to Mika as she sat in the rocking chair. He scooted closer on the couch, so close their knees touched. Annela crossed her legs to escape his.

"So, how long have you been home?" Annela asked.

"About a month," Mika said.

A long silence followed. "What was it like in Norway?"

Mika considered. "The weather is similar to Finland. It has more mountains, though."

Annela eyed the door, trying to conceal her discomfort. She kept waiting for Sister Henderson to come relieve her, though she tried valiantly not to look toward the kitchen for any sign of the lady.

"I hear you went to the university," Mika said after a long pause that Annela simply couldn't manage to fill.

Annela nodded. "Yes, I did. I still have a year left on my master's, but I plan to go back as soon as I have the money." She wondered if he had chosen *Lukio* for his secondary education instead of opting for a technical school after the middle grades. Perhaps he'd gone to college after *Lukio*. "What about you?"

"Oh, school never was my thing. I had no desire to go to *Lukio*. Never did well in anything. Well, except reading."

"You enjoy literature?" Annela asked, clinging to the shred of conversation like a man overboard holds to a lifeline.

His shoulders rose and fell. "I don't know. My teachers thought I was good at it. I did a lot of reading in school." He leaned his leg against hers, making it impossible for Annela to move the rocking chair back and forth to ease her frustration. She could hardly believe he had been home only a month. How had he acted with Norwegian girls on his mission?

"So . . . do you have a favorite author?" Annela asked.

He stared at her with a blank look. For a moment she wondered if he had heard her, and she almost repeated the question when he finally answered, "Oh, I haven't read enough to have one. Just what I had to for school, and that was some time ago."

"I see." Annela knew the food had to be ready; Sister Henderson never put things off to the last minute, always timing everything well ahead of schedule. She was simply giving the two of them more time to hit it off, Annela supposed—but she was ready to die.

"You have gorgeous hair," Mika said.

"Uh, thanks," Annela said, then hurriedly changed subjects. "Did you ever read *Seitsemän Veljestä*?"

Mika sat back a bit in thought. He didn't seem to notice that Annela had pulled away. "*Seitsemän Veljestä* . . ." He paused. "Who wrote it?"

Annela swallowed hard, hiding her reaction to his not remembering one of their country's most renowned authors. "Alexis Kivi."

Mika's head bobbed. "Oh yeah. I read it. But I didn't get it. You know the scene where the brothers get caught on the rock with all the—what were they, bears or cows or whatever—surrounding them? I would have been able to get away without killing them. Or I could have outrun them." He grinned, bobbing his head.

"Really?" Annela couldn't find anything else to say in response, and they lapsed into silence. "I'd better check on Sister Henderson. See what's keeping her." She jumped up, escaping once more to the kitchen.

When Annela entered the kitchen, Sister Henderson glanced over and frowned. "What are you doing in here?" she asked, coming after Annela with a wooden spoon.

"Can we please eat now?"

"But you've hardly had a chance—"

"Please? It's so awkward out there."

Sister Henderson sighed with the air of a martyr. "Fine. We'll eat." She went to call Mika in, but Annela stopped her.

"Sister Henderson?" The elderly woman turned with raised eyebrows, and Annela went on. "If dinner is awkward, please don't make him stay all evening."

"And if dinner goes swimmingly?"

"Then we can talk to him all night for all I care. Agreed?"

"Agreed."

Sister Henderson finally served dinner. Even though Mika was as painful to listen to during the meal as he had been for their previous conversation, dinner was somewhat more bearable. Sister Henderson kept the conversation alive between refilling plates, so Annela no longer had to rack her brain for possible topics. She still had to choke through his comments about how silly composer Jean Sibelius had been to install wooden rain gutters in his house just because they sounded more melodic than metal ones. Mika even wondered why the man was revered for his musical accomplishments.

"Why do we have a monument for him, anyway?" he asked. "And such a ridiculous looking one, too. A bunch of silver pipes floating in the air." Annela bit her tongue, trying not to lash out in defense of another national hero, and even managed to calm herself down when Mika finally admitted he didn't "get" artsy stuff. That was one thing Tommi had going for him; he and Annela loved reading together, going to concerts, and discussing art. She couldn't imagine enjoying anything with Mika. He wasn't her type at all.

Mika didn't offer to help clean up dinner, and Sister Henderson insisted on doing the dishes without Annela's help.

"You two go into the living room and talk," she said. Mika headed out without a backward glance.

"You promised," Annela said accusingly. "Dinner was terrible. I can't handle another minute of this."

Sister Henderson looked sincerely disappointed. "It's that bad?" Annela nodded. "Can you survive just five more minutes? Let me at least clear the table."

"Thank you," Annela said, giving her a squeeze.

Those five minutes felt closer to fifty. When Annela stopped trying to keep up the conversation, Mika actually brought up a topic—hockey. She didn't know a whole lot about the sport aside from what she had observed at skating rinks with the boys in her grade school classes, but she didn't learn much from him, either. He discussed games Annela hadn't seen in vocabulary she didn't understand. About the time Annela's eyes began to glaze over, Sister Henderson came in and thanked Mika for coming to dinner. She managed to politely usher him to the door. When it closed, Annela breathed a sigh of relief.

Sister Henderson turned to her. "Well, what do you think?

"You know what I think," Annela said, going into the kitchen for a seat.

"Annela, but why?" Sister Henderson put her hands in sudsy water and scrubbed a plate.

"We have nothing in common. He can't even carry on an intelligent conversation."

"I was afraid of that. But he's so handsome that I had to hope," Sister Henderson said, rinsing the dish and placing it on the drying rack above the sink. "I must admit that once he opened his mouth he wasn't exactly Prince Charming, was he?" She sounded disappointed at the discovery.

Annela smiled. "No, not exactly."

"But he is a good member."

Annela had to acquiesce on that point, but she still shook her head. "I couldn't ever be interested in him that way, member or not."

Sister Henderson sighed as she put another plate up to dry. She closed the drying rack doors and wiped her hands on a dishrag, then sat down at the table and reached for Annela's hands. "I know the idea of marrying someone you don't even find attractive doesn't seem much like the fairy tales or movies, does it?"

"Not exactly."

Sister Henderson looked from her hands to Annela's face. Her usually cheery eyes were somber. "I joined the Church several years after getting married. My husband never followed. I tried to be patient in hopes that he would eventually come around, but he never did. Don't get me wrong, my Pekka was a good man, and we loved each other dearly. But he never understood why I needed the Church. He didn't understand why I read my scriptures every night, why I prayed, went to church, paid tithing. Tithing. Oh, that was an argument we had more than once." She shook her head wistfully.

"What I am trying to tell you, Annela, is that there are more important things than romance. Blessings to be had which I didn't get. Only after Pekka died eight years ago was I able to go to the temple. Oh, how I wanted to go years before that. I wept the night the ward group left for the Stockholm temple dedication. I wanted to be there so much, but he wouldn't hear of it. He said we couldn't afford the trip, but we both knew better. I never knew if I would be able to step through the temple doors in my lifetime."

Her eyes grew misty. "It was very lonely going to church by myself every week, wanting to bring our daughter, but Pekka not allowing her to come. For years I wished desperately that mine could be one of the eternal families the Primary children sang about. I longed to share my deepest feelings with my husband. I do not want you to live through the same things. You should have a life full of the gospel at every turn. You should be sealed to your husband, watch him bless your children and go home teaching—and to have him at your side at sacrament meeting." Her focus had shifted to the tablecloth, but now she looked up with conviction. "Tommi cannot give you those things, Annela."

Annela wanted to protest, to tell her that he was taking the discussions, that soon he might very well be baptized. And a year after that they could be sealed in the temple. But something stopped her, and she remained silent. Sister Henderson took Annela's hands between her own and her smile returned, only a gentler version than Annela had seen before.

"I just want you to have the happiness you deserve. Promise me you will not marry unless you can be sealed to your husband."

Annela bit her lip, but finally sighed and said, "I promise."

Sister Henderson patted her hands with satisfaction as she stood. "Good. That's all I needed to hear." She wiped her eyes and returned to the sink, where she opened the doors to the racks and began scrubbing dishes.

"But Sister Henderson?" The elderly lady turned around, unaware she was dripping water onto the floor. "No more matchmaking?" Annela finished.

Sister Henderson laughed. "Very well. I'll leave that business up to the Lord."

* * *

Annela saw Tommi only once the rest of the week, although he called several times each day to ask what she was doing, what her schedule was for the day, and what her plans would be for the next. He sounded irritated whenever she didn't know for sure when she'd be free, and since job hunting rarely fit into a tidy schedule, that happened a lot. She felt guilty when she heard him breathing with irritation on the other end, and she assumed he was upset because he had something planned for them, and she'd blown it. Somehow they managed to find a few free hours here and there and planned to meet. But for most of the week he phoned each time to cancel, saying he had been called into work or something else had come up.

Which, Annela thought, was just as well. She still didn't know what to say to him about the Church. She knew she should stay quiet and let him work out his own testimony, but she knew herself too well for that. It didn't take much for her to become a mother hen, poking around and digging for information, and the last thing Tommi needed was extra pressure. On Friday, when she saw him briefly, she ached to ask a dozen questions, but appeased herself by asking one, how far he had read in the Book of Mormon. He seemed a little irritated at her probing.

"I'm getting there," he'd said. "I don't read as fast as you do, you know. I've read up to the dream part you showed me earlier." Annela had nodded, trying not to ask more.

Then he called early Sunday morning, which surprised Annela. He generally slept in on Sundays.

"Hey, how's my girl doing?" he asked.

At first all that registered was that she was hearing Tommi's voice. "Tommi? Is that you? Why are you calling at this hour?"

"Well, I could just hang up if you'd rather."

"No, no," she said, laughing.

"I was just wondering if I could go to church with you today. Figured I'd feel a bit awkward going alone. You could show me around the place, where to go and all that."

Annela's eyes flew open, and she sat up in bed, pushing a tangle of hair from her face. "Really? I mean, sure. That would be great."

She could hear the little noise he always made when he smiled. "It's at ten-thirty, right? I'll come pick you up at fifteen after."

From the moment they entered the building, Tommi was a perfect gentleman. He captivated every *mummo* with his charm and even sent a few blushing with his compliments. Sister Henderson, who opted to take the bus rather than go with them, was gracious and smiling as always, but acted slightly distant. When Tommi noticed the handful of single men standing in the hallway, he pulled Annela in tightly with his arm. She smiled to herself. He was protecting her, sending out the message to potential competition that she belonged to him. It felt good.

They made their way down the hallway to the chapel door, where a man unknown to Annela shook hands with the members as if he were an old friend. He spoke with an accent, although his Finnish was good. He didn't stumble over words or endings, and he knew colloquialisms most missionaries never picked up. His hair was brown with glints of chestnut in it, a color Annela had not seen except on a British movie actor. His well-defined eyebrows framed eyes which warmed with genuine pleasure at the sight of each *mummo* who stopped to fawn over him.

When Sister Henderson saw him, she squealed. She went to her tiptoes, threw her arms about his neck, and planted a kiss on his cheek. Then she turned to Annela. "This is Elder Warner. What's your first name, Elder? I don't think I ever knew it."

He smiled widely at Sister Henderson. "It's Kenneth, although most Finns call me Ken to avoid saying the 'th' at the end."

Sister Henderson's eyes glittered. "Elder—I mean *Ken*—was a missionary a few years back. One of my boys." She turned to him. "Ken, this is Annela. She was just baptized. She's living with me for a while."

Kenneth held out his hand. "Nice to meet you, Annela."

"Nice to meet you, too."

Kenneth put out his hand to Tommi.

"I'm Tommi Fagerlund." They shook hands, a little stiffly on Tommi's part.

"Good to meet you," Kenneth said.

"So Elder, what brought you back?" Sister Henderson said. "Did you miss us so horribly that you just couldn't stay away?"

Kenneth laughed lightly. "Actually, I'm working on my doctorate now, and I came back to do research on my dissertation. It's about the *Kalevala*."

"What could you possibly be studying to make you write about that in America?"

"European literature," he said. "The *Kalevala* is a significant piece of work."

Sister Henderson laughed. "So even in your schooling you couldn't leave us behind."

He shrugged. "I have always loved Europe and its history. And since my mission I've been fascinated by the Finnish people. I'll be here through August, and after that I'll head back to BYU to finish school."

"You'll be here all summer? In that case, I'll have a few months to fatten you up again." She poked his flat stomach. "Since you went ahead and lost all traces of my dinners."

He laughed and patted his belly. "Thanks to you I left the mission a little softer than I arrived. I'll have to be more careful this time, although I doubt I'll be able to resist your desserts." He turned to Annela and Tommi and said, "She makes one incredible strawberry-rhubarb *kiisseli.*" Sister Henderson promised to make him a whole pot of the fruity dessert and entered the chapel to find herself a seat.

Tommi quickly led Annela to a bench in the chapel. He sat down and pulled her close with a firm arm. Feeling impolite for getting rushed off, Annela glanced back at the former missionary apologetically and caught him eyeing her, a smile breaking over his face.

Tommi noticed the interchange. "What was that all about?"

"What was what?"

"Was he trying to flirt with you? As if he can't see you're with me. If he bothers you again, let me know. I'll set him straight."

Annela smiled and looked up at Tommi. "Not getting jealous, are we?"

But Tommi's jaw was clenched, and Annela realized the incident touched a raw nerve. "He'd better not mess with me and what is mine, that's all."

"He was just being friendly, Tommi. Americans are friendly people."

Tommi didn't answer, but she held his hand tightly to comfort him anyway, to let him know he wasn't being threatened in any way by this newcomer. The bishop stood to begin the meeting, and Kenneth Warner slipped down the aisle to a side pew and sat beside Sister Henderson. When the organ began playing the sacrament hymn, Annela leaned over to explain to Tommi what would happen during the sacrament. As she whispered to Tommi, she noticed Kenneth whispering to Sister Henderson, who smiled and nodded, then pulled out a piece of paper and wrote on it. The American tucked the note into his pocket. Sister Henderson glanced back at Annela, a silly grin on her face. Annela wished she could be a fly on Sister Henderson's shoulder to see what was in that note.

Annela took the bread and water with gratitude in her heart. The experience was still new, one that she wouldn't take for granted any time soon. She wished her mother could have been baptized with her, could partake with her.

As the first speaker began, Annela noticed the bookmark in Tommi's Book of Mormon, which lay on his lap with its top facing her. The little green paper had to be significantly past First Nephi. Tommi's attention was focused on the speaker, so Annela reached over and cracked the pages ever so slightly. Mosiah 14! He must have done a lot of reading the past few days, she thought gleefully. He was not only giving the gospel a try, but if he was already halfway through Mosiah, he was feeling the truth of the book, she felt sure of it.

Mosiah 14—she opened her own scriptures and flipped to the chapter. He had just read the story of Abinadi, one of her favorites, and one of the most powerful. Annela scanned through the next chapters. Tommi would come to the story of Alma soon. Alma, the one priest of Noah who listened to Abinadi and saw the truth for what it was. Who wasn't afraid of public opinion. Tommi resembled Alma in that way.

If that story didn't move him, there were always dozens of others he would reach soon. Annela put her scriptures aside and took his hand in hers. She couldn't help squeezing Tommi's hand periodically in excitement over what she just knew must be happening within him.

CHAPTER 6

"I have a job!" Annela announced, slamming the door victoriously behind her.

"That's terrific," Sister Henderson said from her rocking chair. She discarded her knitting without finishing the row and hurried into the entryway where Annela was hanging her jacket. She gave her a big hug, then added, "I think I still have some ice cream. Let's celebrate."

Sister Henderson opened the fridge and lifted the compact door to the freezer section. Inside she found a liter of ice cream—vanilla with a heart-shaped, strawberry-flavored core. She sliced it into blocks, deposited two in each bowl, and placed one before Annela, who had already taken a seat at the table. Annela shoveled a spoonful into her mouth.

Sister Henderson replaced the ice cream carton, wiped her sticky fingers on a dishrag, and sat down at the table. "Now, tell me the whole story from the beginning. I don't suppose you found an office job after all?"

"No, I wasn't that lucky. Maybe in a few months if the economy improves. I pretty much exhausted downtown Helsinki stores, so I decided to try the Itäkeskus mall."

"Did you apply at Marimekko?"

"Yes, but they aren't hiring. Neither was the shoe store, the book store, or three clothing stores I tried. I had almost given up when I decided to get something to eat at the Hansa Bridge snack window."

"So you're working there?"

Annela smiled at Sister Henderson's eagerness. "No, not that either. But I overheard two women talking about needing to hire

someone quickly at The Candy Bag. I approached them, one inter-
viewed me, and I got the job."

Sister Henderson's face lit up. "I wonder if you could get a
discount on chocolate."

Annela chuckled and took another bite of ice cream. "Maybe."

When the phone rang, Annela stood to answer it. "You better
start eating before your ice cream turns into just cream," she told
Sister Henderson, heading for the phone on the end table in the
entryway.

"Hello, Henderson residence," Annela said, licking ice cream off
her finger.

"Annela? Annela, is that you?" a female voice almost whispered.

Annela's hand gripped the phone so she wouldn't drop it. "Mom?"
Although she hadn't seen or heard from her mother since the baptism,
Annela thought about her mother and sister all the time, worried
about them. "Mom, are you all right?"

"We're fine," she said. Annela noticed she hadn't said "I." She
spoke softly. "I just needed to call you, to see how you're doing. I
worry about you."

"And I worry about you," Annela said, leaning against the
doorway to her room. "Did Dad find out that you came to my
baptism?"

She spoke quickly. "Well, yes. But I'm fine. We're fine. Everything's
okay."

Her rush to assure Annela had just the opposite effect. Annela
heard loud motor sounds and voices in the background and knew her
mother was calling from a pay phone. She understood without any
explanation. If Dad were to find out she had made even this contact
with his "dead daughter" . . . Annela cringed and tried not to think
about it.

"I doubt I'll be able to visit you at your apartment," Helena went
on. "But I do wish I could see you."

Annela understood her mother's hidden meanings. Her father
wouldn't allow an excursion to visit her, and he would watch the
bus stop to see which direction his wife went, from which direction
she came home, how much time and money she spent. It had better
add up.

"I got a job in the mall," Annela said. "At The Candy Bag. I start on Wednesday, but I don't know for sure what my work schedule will be."

"Great. I'll see you when I can. Kirsti needs a new pair of shoes, so I'll go there soon." Her voice was quiet, and Annela could tell she was on the verge of tears. "Well, I have to go. I'll see you later."

"Okay."

Annela almost hung up, when Helena choked out, "I love you, Annela. Bye."

After a stunned second, Annela said, "I love you too, Mom," but was unsure whether her mother had heard it.

Annela held the phone in her hand and stroked the smooth plastic with her thumb. She had never heard those words from her mother before. She had read it on her mother's card, but hearing them struck her to the center. Annela's hand shook as she replaced the receiver, her knees threatening to buckle.

Sister Henderson came behind Annela and placed a hand on her shoulder. Grateful for her soft hand, Annela turned and fell into her hug.

"Is everything all right at home?" Sister Henderson asked.

Annela nodded, then looked at her. "She said she loves me." Annela smiled through her tears. Her lips quivered, and she attempted to calm them with a trembling hand. Sister Henderson pulled Annela close again and stroked her hair. Annela felt like the little girl clutching her Geisha bar Christmas morning, clinging to it as a sign that someone cared. But this time she *knew* that someone did.

Her mother had said so.

* * *

Tommi had another appointment with the missionaries on Tuesday. Annela would be coming again, but he had something else planned first. He told her to meet him at Elephant Rock an hour before the appointment, but he arrived twenty minutes before that to set up. After spreading a tablecloth on the flattest part of the rocky protrusion, he began to set up a picnic lunch.

As he organized the picnic, he thought about Annela. He didn't know how much longer he could keep seeing the missionaries before she started pressuring him about getting baptized. Tommi almost wished he could feel the same way Annela did about the Mormons and their church. It all sounded well and good, but how could one really know? And he, for one, wasn't willing to sacrifice his Sundays, his occasional wine, or a tenth of his hard-earned money. But he loved Annela. Really loved her. And he would do almost anything to keep her.

He stood and surveyed the meal. With a nod of satisfaction, he turned to face the melting sea while he waited for Annela. The ice no longer reached the shore, and daily the edges thinned a little more. He took a deep breath and hoped that his efforts to keep Annela's heart would work now that they no longer shared a home. With any luck she would accept his efforts to understand her new life, even if he couldn't join her in it.

"What's all this?" Annela asked, approaching from behind.

Tommi turned around and reached for her hand. "Just a little surprise. It's been a while since we had much quality time together." He led Annela to the blanket where they sat down. It was just large enough for the two of them and the basket of food. The wind kicked up the blanket again and again, so Tommi had to keep fixing it. Eventually he hunted rocks to hold down each corner.

"That should do it," he said, sitting beside Annela again. He reached into the basket and withdrew a small glass vase with a white rose. Annela bit her lower lip, clearly pleased. Tommi grinned. This would work. It had to.

"The rose is our centerpiece," he said. "Although it hardly looks pretty when you're beside it."

Sandwiches and little bags of fruit came next. He gave Annela hers first and even unwrapped her sandwich. Tommi reached into the basket again and pushed a button on the mini boom box inside. Soft music wafted through the air. It was the first song they had ever danced to—"Smoke Gets in Your Eyes." Annela held her sandwich in both hands and looked at him with feigned protest.

Tommi scooted a little closer and drew another blanket around the two of them to keep out the breeze. "I hope I'm sweeping the most beautiful woman in the world off her feet." He gently brushed a stray wisp of hair from her eyes. The wind put it right back, but he brushed it away again and looked deeply into her eyes. "Is it working?"

Annela nodded.

"Good." Tommi opened a package of cookies and lifted one as if to feed it to her. She opened her mouth as if to protest, but when Tommi shook his head, Annela submitted to his touch. He had heard enough about her childhood to know that affection was not something in large supply, but it was something he had plenty to give. The more she accepted, the more Tommi would give.

After finishing off the last crumbs from the cookie box, they sat close to each other and watched the tiny waves trying to break through thin, melting ice. Tommi let the silence work its magic before talking. When he finally spoke it was with intensity.

"I need you, Annela. I really need you." He turned to her and took her hand in his. He gently traced its edges with one finger as he would a priceless statue. "I can't live without you."

Annela began to speak, then stopped when her voice cracked. "Really?"

Tommi nodded. "I want to be part of your life forever." Tommi looked into her eyes, grateful that so far she seemed to accept his words. He took a moment before going on, knowing he was about to tell her something he had never spoken to anyone, not even Annela. But he had to tell her now. It was the only way to make her understand his love for her, his desperate need for her.

"When I was a little kid, maybe seven or eight, my parents fought all the time. I remember crying myself to sleep at night, trying to ignore the walls shaking as Mom and Dad yelled at each other. Then I'd have nightmares that they'd get a divorce. But every time I asked them about it, they went on and on—'How could I imagine such a thing? They would never leave each other, never leave me.' They promised that they'd never leave, over and over again. And I believed them."

"But they did divorce," Annela said quietly.

Tommi nodded. "Dad went away, and Mom was such a wreck she might as well have gone too." He swallowed a knot in his throat, then stared into the sky and blinked hard.

"I'm so sorry," Annela murmured.

He turned to her, his heart aching as he relived the pain of those days. "The only people I've ever let myself love have abandoned me, broken their promises to me. They have all left."

"Tommi, I had no idea," Annela said, reaching up to touch his cheek. "I had no idea your parents' divorce affected you so strongly. You always acted as if it didn't."

"I know," he said with a cynical smile. "I decided not to let anyone get too close, so I wouldn't love them, then get hurt again." He looked out at the miniature island as if he could see the ocean beyond it. His lower lip quivered, and he felt a tear forming at the corner of his eye. He blinked hard and it fell, making a shining streak down one cheek as he looked back at her.

"But now, in spite of myself, I love you, Annela. You could snap my heart in two if you wanted." *Please don't,* he thought. *I need you too much to be hurt again.*

"I would never do anything to hurt you, you know that." Annela dried his cheek with her finger, warming his skin. He had missed her touch more than he knew. He reached up and held her hand to his cheek.

Tommi's eyes were both blurry now. He blinked again, and a few drops tumbled down his cheeks. "Do you love me, Annela?"

"Tommi, we've known each other for half of our lives."

"I know, but do you love me?" he asked, pressing the issue as he held her hands in his.

"Of course I love you," she said. "You are part of me that I will carry in my heart for the rest of my life."

He pulled back, his fears of losing Annela resurfacing. "'Carry in your heart?' That sounds as if you're planning on leaving me behind."

"No, no, of course not," she said hastily. "I just mean that you'll always be a part of me. No matter what the future holds, I'll always care for you."

He held her hand tighter. "Promise you'll never leave me behind?"

"I promise." She kissed him soundly, calming his fears. Tommi wiped at his eyes with the back of his hand. Annela grinned. "Now it's your turn to have a red nose."

Tommi laughed out loud. "Oh yeah? Do you know what you deserve for that crack?" He pounced in her direction and threatened to tickle her, but instead wrapped his arms about Annela and kissed her hard. He again brushed at a stray lock of hair. "If only I could see your face every day for the rest of my life."

Annela shook her head in disbelief. Tommi raised his eyebrows. "What?"

She waved him off. "Nothing. It's just that I've always imagined what it would be like to hear those kinds of words. I thought they were only in the movies, and now someone is actually saying them to me. Little ol' Annela with the stringy hair." She tossed a straggly section to the side.

"With the hair of silk," Tommi corrected, stroking it.

"That is exactly what I mean! I keep wanting to pinch myself. This isn't a dream, is it?"

Tommi tilted her chin toward him and kissed her tenderly. "It's more real than anything *I've* ever felt."

* * *

When they returned to Tommi's apartment to meet the missionaries, Annela glanced in the mirror and saw that her cheeks were pink. She looked down at the white rose in her hand, which Tommi had given to her as a memento of the day, then back at her reflection. The rose was beautiful with its velvety white petals. Tommi had said she was more beautiful than the rose. She thought of all the stinging remarks her father had made about her looks, saying her mother was to blame for them.

Annela should have been a beautiful child like Kirsti. But she was ugly. And she believed it. Even now, with Tommi's rose in her hand, she had trouble accepting the fact that anyone could think her pretty. She grasped the rose tightly, unwilling to give the moment a chance for escape. A thorn pricked her finger, and she realized she had clung a little too tightly. A deep crimson drop appeared on the tip of her finger and stained the white petals. The spell was broken, and she went in search of a bandage.

When the missionaries gave the next discussion, they were stunned to see Tommi's bookmark tucked at the third chapter of Alma.

"You read all the way through Mosiah this week?" Elder Stevens asked.

Tommi looked at the bookmark. "Well, yeah. It's pretty interesting."

"Except Second Nephi, right?" Elder Densley said with a chuckle. "That's usually where most investigators choke."

"Of course. Except that part," was all Tommi said with a forced chuckle.

Elder Stevens then followed up on Tommi's promise to pray about what he had been reading. Annela mentally crossed her fingers and waited for his answer.

"Yes, I've been praying about it," he said.

When he didn't elaborate, Elder Stevens probed further. "Have you felt the Spirit testify of its truthfulness?"

Tommi paused for a moment as if to choose the right words. Annela held her breath. "Well, I do feel good when I read it, but no, I don't know yet whether it's true."

The elders nodded and said something about how the witness would come if he sincerely sought it, and then continued on with the discussion. Annela tried not to feel disappointed. After all, he had read up to Alma, hadn't he? That had to mean something.

The missionaries seemed pleased with his progress as they went on with the next discussion. Annela remembered Elder Densley challenging her to baptism at the end of their second visit. But Tommi wasn't ready for that yet, and the elders seemed to sense it. They once again skipped over the challenge for baptism, but said that they hoped by their next visit Tommi would have received his witness and be ready to commit to a date.

Tommi flashed his charming smile. "I'll do my best," he said. "I'll keep reading and praying. That's all I can do, right?"

After the missionaries left, Annela retrieved her purse from the end table and slipped her shoes on.

"Going already?" Tommi asked.

Annela looked at his disappointed eyes. "I can't stay. I'm sorry, but I promised Sister Henderson I'd help her prepare food for the ward's *Vappu* party on Friday. She's making two dozen cakes for it."

"All right, fine then. Just go. Leave me. Forget all about me. I knew you'd break your promise."

Annela knew he was speaking in jest, but his reference to her promise stung. Another part of her sensed that inside him was the little boy who had been let down by his parents, and he still needed reassurance. After slinging her purse over her shoulder, she crossed to him.

"I don't break promises, Tommi. I have to go now, but that doesn't mean I'm leaving you behind, and you know it. In fact," she said, brightening, "do you want to come to the *Vappu* party with me? I won't have to help serve except at the beginning, and if Sister Henderson has anything to do with it, I won't get a chance to step inside the kitchen at all. I know a Mormon party is not exactly what you're used to doing for the holiday, but it'll be fun. It's a dance." She threw that last part in because she knew the idea of dancing might tip the scales in her favor. The two of them had taken a few dance classes together and used the skill as often as they could.

Vappu was always a rowdy celebration in Finland, and Annela looked forward to spending it with sober members instead of out in the city, barely avoiding the drunks that seemed to be on every street corner. *Vappu* scared Annela sometimes with its focus on alcohol. At home it had always been a day to dread. She would sit in the apartment with her mother and sister, sipping glasses of the traditional *Vappu* drink, *sima*, while awaiting her father's return and bracing themselves for his drunken outbursts. Her mother usually had bruises the first week of May.

"*Vappu?*" Tommi said with surprise. "Oh, that's right. Friday is May first." His shoulders slumped. "I'm sorry, Annela. I forgot about *Vappu*. No wonder everyone at work wanted Friday off. I didn't think anything of it, so I promised to cover for the assistant manager. But you go to the party and have fun. Just don't dance with too many guys. I might get jealous."

CHAPTER 7

Friday night Annela donned one of Sister Henderson's flowery aprons and bustled about the ward-house kitchen, obeying directions tossed at her from the *mummos*. A low murmur grew in the hall as guests arrived and milled around. Soon the lights in the cultural hall dimmed and music started. Some fifteen minutes later, Sister Henderson appeared behind Annela.

"It's time you get out there," she said as she fought with the knot on Annela's apron.

Annela turned to protest. "But you still need me at least for a few minutes. I promise I'll go out as soon as the first rush is over."

Sister Henderson raised an eyebrow as if Annela were challenging her authority. She turned Annela back around by the shoulders and resumed tugging at the defiant knot. "You've done your share of helping. Goodness, you've been nothing but a flurry of apron ruffles since we got here. It's time for you to go out and socialize." When the tie finally released its hold, Sister Henderson victoriously removed the apron and waved Annela toward the door.

"But—"

"But nothing. Go, go, go."

In no time Annela found herself standing alone in the hallway and feeling every inch awkward. She silently wished Tommi could have come. Parties were well and good as long as she had someone to be with. Standing by the wall with another person wasn't at all embarrassing, but meandering alone and attempting small talk with paired couples was. Annela had a shy streak that came out when familiar security blankets weren't around. Take that person away, and she froze.

She stood in the doorway for a few minutes, trying to decide which would be more humiliating, being on display for every arriving person to pity, or vainly attempting to dissolve into the crowd, but sticking out anyway. She decided on the latter and entered the cultural hall, where the walls were lined three people deep. So far no one had ventured onto the dance floor. Instead they talked at the edges of the room, most holding glasses of *sima*. A song ended, and the emcee informed the crowd about refreshments in the kitchen.

Another song began, but the crowd moved as a single mind toward the kitchen. Annela found herself on the verge of getting trampled, so she ducked toward the stage to avoid the river of people. Discreetly out of the way, she tried to look busy by pouring a cup of *sima* at a nearby table. She took a sip of the fizzy lemon drink and watched the floating raisins.

"I think Sister Henderson's refreshments are a bigger hit than anything else."

Annela jumped at the sudden voice and sloshed punch onto her hand, narrowly avoiding a mess on her white blouse. Kenneth Warner stood a few feet away with his own cup and pointed toward the kitchen. "Maybe some sugar will help to liven the party a bit, or at least get some people onto the dance floor."

Annela glanced his way and then at the kitchen as she fumbled with some napkins to wipe her hand off before she dripped *sima* onto the floor. "Yeah, maybe."

People began trickling back into the room, but the dance floor remained vacant. A song finished, and still no one danced. Annela's feet itched to take the floor. But even if Tommi were there, she knew they wouldn't be dancing yet. She never allowed Tommi to take them out first.

"Hmm . . ." Kenneth said with a smile playing about the corners of his mouth.

"What?" Annela asked, curious as to what thought had provoked the expression.

"It's just that—don't take this wrong or anything—Finns tend to be afraid of sticking out. If they could fill the dance floor without anyone noticing them, it would be packed right now."

"No offense taken. And you're right. We could spend the whole night just staring out from the sides of the room, and no one would bother to be the first couple. I don't blame them, really. I wouldn't mind so much being the second or third even, but the first?" Annela shook her head. "I couldn't do that."

Kenneth held out his hand for her empty cup, and Annela assumed he was offering to refill it. To her dismay, he placed both cups on the stage behind him, took her hand, and made for the center of the room. Annela choked on a protest, and even tried to slip her hand away, but to no avail. Kenneth either didn't notice or didn't care, and soon she found herself the center of attention, all eyes on her and the American. He turned around and held up his hands in dance position, waiting for hers.

"What dances do you know?" he asked. "I heard from a reliable source that you have taken classes. I'm sure I'm not nearly as good a partner as you're used to, but I know a few steps."

Annela flushed, knowing Sister Henderson must have been the "source" and wondering what else she had told him. "This song would be good for a cha-cha," she finally said, surrendering herself to humiliation, as she saw no other option.

"Cha-cha it is." He began leading her through several basic steps. She couldn't help but compare Kenneth to Tommi, and to her chagrin, Tommi came up short. Not that Kenneth was more experienced—he wasn't. He didn't know a lot of steps, and his technique had a few obvious beginner flaws. But he led better than Tommi. And Kenneth was quite a bit taller, which put him at just the right height for Annela, making it easier for her to follow. Annela had always thought she and Tommi were a little too close in height to do well as dance partners.

Annela's thoughts continued in the same vein, and she was unaware of her fading embarrassment until it was gone and she was enjoying herself. She fervently hoped her face hadn't turned red; embarrassment had a similar effect to that of crying. Kenneth released her hand to lead into a walk-around turn, and as she came around to take his hands again, she noticed several young women on the edges of the room eyeing them with envy.

With a grin, Kenneth released Annela's hand and turned away to begin "the chase." She grinned back and "chased" him, then turned around and led the chase as he pursued. When she came around the next time, she caught Sister Henderson standing at the doorway with a dishtowel in her hands and a twinkle in her eye. Annela would have sent Sister Henderson a chastising look for breaking her match-making promise if Annela hadn't been enjoying herself so much. When the song ended, Annela made a move to leave the floor, but Kenneth held her hand and didn't leave.

"Do you know the samba?" he asked when the next song began. Annela nodded, and away they went again. They danced to the next song, and then Kenneth graciously led Annela off the floor. As they walked toward the drink table, she heard a few disappointed comments float out and she smiled inwardly. The crowd had enjoyed watching them. Several other couples had joined Kenneth and Annela, and as the two of them left, some followed them off the floor and other couples replaced them. The dance was under way.

When they returned to the stage, Annela noticed that Kenneth's forehead sparkled with a few tiny drops and his breathing was a little faster. He reached for her empty cup and refilled it.

"You're very good," he said, holding her drink out for her to take.

"Thank you," Annela managed, flushing horribly as she took the cup. So much for not turning red. She never could take compliments well, but this was ridiculous. Annela could hardly speak around this American, and she felt her stomach flip-flopping constantly. She shouldn't have missed dinner, she realized. She wouldn't feel so weak if she hadn't.

"What other dances do you know?" Kenneth asked between swallows. "Personally, I love waltzes, but I rarely hear them anymore."

"Me too," Annela said, an awkward smile cracking her lips. "I always want to request a waltz at dances, but the Latin ones are more Tommi's—" She stopped, suddenly realizing that mentioning a boyfriend right then wouldn't exactly make anyone comfortable.

"Tommi? Is that the man who was with you at church?"

Annela nodded and sipped her punch absently, trying to look cool and collected.

"Where is he tonight?"

"At work."

A few more couples had migrated to the dance floor, probably because the song was slow and it gave men without much talent or rhythm an opportunity to dance without embarrassment, not to mention the fact that it was a good excuse for young couples to be romantic. Part of Annela wanted to be back on the dance floor, and the other half chided herself for even thinking about dancing to a slow song with anyone but Tommi.

Kenneth casually set aside his empty cup and watched the dance floor for a minute. Annela did the same. The silence grew awkward, but she didn't know what to say. Kenneth turned to her.

"Care to?"

Without a word Annela took his hand, and once again he led the way to the dance floor. She expected Kenneth to assume the "loose hug" position all the other couples had, but instead was pleasantly surprised when he took a relaxed version of the traditional dance position. Kenneth led them around in a gentle circle, and again she saw envious faces of the other single women, including a few Laurels.

When they rotated to the west doors, Annela saw Tommi standing in the doorway. With the hall lights behind him she couldn't make out the expression on his face, but when he saw Annela, she knew it. His stance tightened, and he entered with a determined but none-too-stable stride, directly for her and Kenneth. A few steps into the room she could see the fury on his face. He had to steady himself a few times against tables on his way, but he never took his eyes off her. Kenneth heard her quick intake of breath.

"Is something wrong?" he asked, dropping their arms. He turned to look where Annela's gaze was fixed.

When Tommi reached them, the stale smell of alcohol hit Annela like a dirty cloud. She braced herself by tightening her grip on Kenneth's hand, a gut reaction to the smell of her father coming home drunk. Tommi had never smelled that strongly.

"Let go of her!" Tommi barked at Kenneth.

Annela pulled her hand away as if Kenneth's were poison. "Hi, Tommi. What are you doing here?" she asked, trying to sound casual.

"What am *I* doing here?" Tommi repeated, as if she had no right to be speaking to him at all. "What am *I* doing here? What are *you* doing here with him? Trying to find a Mormon man for yourself, you slut?"

The body before her was Tommi, but the face and voice were ones she had never seen. She tried to choke back the hurt and think straight. "Tommi, you knew I was coming tonight. You told me to come and enjoy myself while you worked. Kenneth hasn't done anything but dance with me a few times."

Tommi reached for her arm and pulled her to him. "I don't want you dancing with any smelly Americans." Tommi looked at Kenneth. "She's mine, and I won't have you trying to take her."

"Tommi, calm down," Annela whispered, painfully aware of the gaping crowd. "People are watching." She should have known better; he couldn't have cared less about people watching him when he was sober, and drunkenness certainly wouldn't add discretion to his character.

"I won't calm down for you or any other Mormons!" he yelled, then tightened his grip about her arm. She wanted to yelp in pain, but kept silent. It would be the safer course, even if it meant bruises later. She knew that from experience at home. She turned to him and tried to speak to the man she knew was somewhere inside him.

"It's all right, Tommi. Let's sit down and talk."

He hesitated a moment, glaring at Kenneth, his eyes blazing, but he finally agreed to take a seat at one of the tables on the far end of the cultural hall. Kenneth tried to follow, but Tommi turned on him.

"Stay out of this!" he snapped. Kenneth raised his hands in surrender and backed off, but remained close by. Annela felt a little safer knowing he was watching.

Tommi sat down at the first table he came to and released Annela's arm. His head hung, and he ran his fingers through his already tousled hair, a dejected look on his face. His whole body was lifeless. Annela sat beside him and rested her hand on his arm.

"Tommi? Are you all right?" He didn't respond, just stared in a daze at the table. She figured something must have happened to send him to the bottle. "Tommi, what's wrong? Why have you been drinking?"

Had something happened at the restaurant? It was practically his baby; it was so unlike him to abandon work, especially on a holiday.

His face flushed darker and he lashed out, throwing her hand off his arm. "Can't a man have a drink if he wants to? Of course not. At least, not in a Mormon church. I guess I'm damned now, for coming into a holy house with a few beers in my gut, right?"

Annela sat back with no idea what to say or how to respond. Tommi decided for her. "We're talking outside," he said, grabbing her arm. He stood up and none too gently pulled her out of the cultural hall, down the hallway, and out the church doors. Once outside he released her with a shove and stared her down. The sun had set and the day's light was fading. The night air was crisp; Annela shivered and hugged herself, wishing she had her jacket. But it wasn't really the cold that bothered her. Tommi's menacing expression was what made her shiver.

"Let's sort this all out tomorrow when you're feeling better," she said. "Everything is all right. It really is. You'll see. It's just the alcohol talking."

Tommi whirled around. "It's the alcohol, is it? So of course it's all my fault because you self-righteous Mormons won't drink it." He took two steps to close the distance between them. "You self-righteous whore!" He raised his hand and turned it toward her.

For a moment Annela saw only his hand descending in an arc. With a snap, the back of it struck the side of her face. Her cheek burned, and she covered it with her hand, unwilling to look up at the monster Tommi had become. He had never hit her before. Never.

Kenneth burst out of the doors. "Get away from her!"

Tommi turned on him. "Or what? Are you going to fight me or something?"

Annela had to stifle a gasp as he lunged at Kenneth, stumbling over his own feet in his drunken stupor. Tommi tried to land a punch, which Kenneth easily avoided. He faced Kenneth again, his fists clenched as if ready to fight.

"I suggest you leave," Kenneth said, his feet planted firmly and his fists ready to defend himself. Tommi stopped for a moment. He glared at Annela, then eyed Kenneth as if trying to size up the competition. In his drunken state, Tommi was little match for a sober man, taller and broader than himself, and even he knew it. After what felt like several minutes but was probably only a few seconds, he let out a few curses and finally skulked away down the sidewalk, still cussing.

Kenneth sighed heavily and turned to Annela. "Are you all right?"

"I'll be fine," she said, still in a daze, but fighting the stinging in her eyes. Her hands trembled.

"Tommi may come back," Kenneth said, still watching him in the distance. "It would probably be best for you to go home. Do you want a ride?"

"Yes, thanks," Annela said, then tried to steady her breathing.

"Come on, let's go get your things."

She nodded, and Kenneth led her into the chapel with his hand on her back. She waited inside the doors while he retrieved her jacket and purse. With her right hand still hovering about her stinging cheek, she took a deep breath, her thoughts on the emptiness left in her heart. She turned toward the doors and leaned against them hard as tears pooled in her eyes and fell. So this is what her mother felt like.

CHAPTER 8

Annela cried for hours that night, not giving a thought to the state her face would be in the next morning. At first she cried because the very thing she had sworn years ago would never happen to her had just happened. Then she cried because of what Tommi had become, right in the middle of taking the discussions, right when he had seemed so eager to investigate the Church.

Right before the discussion about the Word of Wisdom, Annela realized with irony.

The thought reminded her of a shoe box under the bed. Inside it, she had stashed the contents of a thick envelope she had requested from Brigham Young University. She hadn't told anyone that she harbored the hope of going there to finish her master's degree someday. She pulled the box out and again looked at the pictures and read course requirements. As usual, she didn't allow herself to read through the admissions application, for fear it would make her yearn for something that would never be. With a sigh, she dropped the papers back into the shoe box and pushed it under the bed. That kind of escape wouldn't be happening.

Through blurred vision, she noticed her Book of Mormon. She swiped at both cheeks, in no mood to read. A tiny voice assured her that she really didn't need to read tonight of all nights. But she fought the impulse to wallow in self-pity and instead picked up the scriptures and opened them to her bookmark. She read in hopes of a verse jumping out at her, maybe even offering an answer to what she should do next. When nothing struck her, she almost felt let down. But at the same time she realized that she was no longer crying, that a calm had entered the room and she could fall sleep in spite of her pounding headache.

At work the next day, Annela ended up taking a late lunch break in the back room because Kaisa, who was supposed to cover during that time, showed up late. When she finally arrived, Annela gratefully went to eat her sandwich and cut-up veggies. Her shoes felt tight from standing all day. Mia, the employee Annela usually worked with, came into the back room.

Mia had features virtually opposite of most Finnish women, ones Annela and her classmates had always envied in other girls. Instead of straight blond hair, Mia's brunette locks had natural waves. Dark lashes framed her brown eyes, and she had olive-toned skin, the kind that tans instead of burns. Mia never wore exactly the same outfit more than once. She would add a scarf or belt, roll up the sleeves, layer shirts, or add a pin to create a slightly different look. Some days Annela felt as if she might as well have been a pale ghost in comparison. Today was even worse, since her face had yet to recover from her stormy night.

Annela groaned inwardly, knowing how she must look to all the customers—a washed out, limp rag. At times Annela had moments of feeling pretty, but working beside Mia tended to make those times few and far between.

Mia picked up her purse and headed for the door, going out for lunch as she always did, but this time she stopped and turned around. "Hey Annela, do you want to join me? I'm going to Clock's. They have the best fish fillets."

In her short time working at The Candy Bag, Annela and Mia had never had much of a working relationship, let alone a friendship of any kind, so she had no idea where this invitation was coming from. She thought it must be from pity, and she opened her mouth to refuse. *Who cares if it is out of pity,* she decided. A fish fillet sounded quite good right now, and besides, she knew Mia would make a fun conversation companion, something she could really use. If nothing else, it would help get her mind off Tommi.

"Sure. I'd love to come."

Annela tucked her lunch away, and soon she and Mia were heading toward Clock's. Mia ordered two fish fillets and a large order of fries for herself. Annela eyed her tiny waist and marveled in half disgust that anyone could eat out every day and still look like that. They went upstairs to the seating area and found a table beside a black-and-white print of a woman with a broad hat shielding her face.

Mia began chattering as soon as she sat down. Annela dug into her french fries, glad Mia was the one doing the talking. She didn't say much of import, but Annela enjoyed lunch nonetheless. Mia jabbered about her latest haircut and debated whether she should highlight her hair again or not. Last time she got highlights, she didn't think they looked good on her, but then, her hair had been shorter and permed, so highlights might look really different now with long, unpermed hair, and what did Annela think? Or maybe she should layer it.

"I think you're beautiful," Annela said, looking up from her sandwich. "You could get dunked in a puddle of mud and come out looking terrific."

Mia shook her head and laughed, sending her hair moving in gentle waves about her face. "You're too nice," she said. "But seriously. What do you think? I just can't make up my mind." Mia licked some ketchup from her fingers and took a hearty bite from her fillet.

"I'm sure highlights would look great," Annela said. "And I'm guessing you'll worry about it until you try it. Then you'll find out whether you think you look good that way. And you'll change it all over again and still look great."

Mia nodded and dipped a french fry in ketchup. "You're right about one thing. I always have a crisis about my hair. Each time I swear I'll never cut it or dye it or perm it again. I always do, anyway, just to satisfy my curiosity."

Annela took a sip of her drink and shook her head. "I guess I'm not much help. It's just that frankly, if I had your skin tone, I wouldn't care how my hair looked."

"You would if you were me," she said, the sparkle in her eyes dying slightly, which belied her sunny tone.

"But look at you! You're so pretty. You have a gorgeous boyfriend. Katrina told me you've been winning music competitions—vocal *and* violin, right?—since you could talk. And didn't you just make it into the Sibelius Music Academy? What more could you want?"

"Sounds pretty great, doesn't it?" Mia's brow furrowed as she made ketchup trails with the end of a french fry. When she spoke it was so soft Annela could hardly hear her. "If it's so wonderful, then why am I not happy? It's as if I'm chasing after . . . something—I don't know what—and never finding it. Sometimes it's just out of reach, and I think I catch it, but then it floats away and I start chasing after it again."

Annela kept quiet now, knowing that Mia needed to speak her thoughts without interruption. Besides, she had no idea what to tell Mia. Her life did seem almost perfect.

Mia looked directly at her. "Annela, have you ever wanted something so badly and then gotten it, only to discover it wasn't so great after all? That's my life over and over again. I have lots of awards from music competitions. Now I'll be going to the academy. I thought I'd finally be happy when I got in. But every time I get something, it never measures up to what I expect it to be. So I keep searching for something else to fill up the empty spot."

"What are you looking for now?" Annela asked.

Mia shrugged. "I don't know. My latest 'accomplishment' was getting Kari for a boyfriend. Now I'm the envy of all my friends. I wanted him to notice me for so long, and when he finally did—well, let's just say for two weeks I thought I had it all." She smiled dubiously.

"And now?"

"And now, it doesn't matter. Kari's not the kind of guy that can make a girl happy. Not for long, anyway. I'm just a trophy he carries around to show off. If I gained five kilos, he wouldn't want to be with me anymore. And I'm getting tired of him, too. He always has a cigarette hanging out of his mouth. I can hardly breathe around him."

Annela's mind turned to her father's rage in refusing to let her come home, to Tommi's anger and his finally hitting her. Was she happy with all of that? The answer surprised her. Those things were hard, sure. But when it came down to deciding if she would trade her life with baptism for one without all her problems—but also without the gospel—she decided she would have it no other way. Granted, with all she was dealing with, she didn't have an overwhelming urge to shout from the rooftops in glee. She had spent the previous night crying, after all. But she could honestly say that she had peace about her life in general, the comfort and calm that only the Holy Ghost can bring, which she had felt last night.

Annela briefly debated whether to bring up the Church, but she didn't feel the time was right to push conversion stories on Mia. Instead, Annela asked if she were much of a religious person. Mia admitted she wasn't. Annela paused and considered her words carefully, praying for guidance.

"Mia, I can tell you about the one thing that hasn't disappointed me, and never will." Mia eyed her curiously, unsure of where she was going with this. "It may sound silly, especially if you're not religious, but trust me—this is something I know from experience. True happiness comes from God's love. Knowing that it is always there, unconditionally. He is there to help, and will never turn away."

Mia's face tilted down, and her hair fell in the way, so Annela couldn't see her reaction. But when she didn't say anything, Annela felt a knot twisting its way through her stomach. She almost apologized for intruding, when Mia finally looked up. Two bright tears trickled down one cheek.

"That sounds too good to be true, Annela. I only wish it applied to me. God doesn't love me. After all I've done, how could He?"

* * *

That night, as Annela brushed her teeth, the doorbell rang. She waited a few minutes to see if Sister Henderson would get the door, but then remembered she was on her evening walk with her neighbor friend from apartment 304. The bathroom mirror showed that washing her face had helped to lessen the puffiness in her eyes, but she still grimaced at the image. She didn't know of anyone else whose eyes stayed swollen so long after crying. It was infuriating.

She ran her fingers through straggling hair, although the effort didn't help much. When the doorbell rang again, Annela pulled on her robe and shuffled over to answer it. The peephole revealed a mass of petals. With a stunned gasp, she opened the door. A huge vase of roses hid the person behind them.

"Delivery," came a voice. Tommi. Annela quickly took the vase from him. "I believe there is a card attached," he said, still attempting to maintain the delivery boy impression. As she placed the vase on the hall end table, the smell wafted about her. She found the card and opened it.

"For the most beautiful woman in the world, from the most despicable and unworthy man in the world," she read aloud.

Tommi took a step over the threshold with clasped hands. His knuckles had turned white from nervousness. Heavy circles of blue ringed his eyes, and his entire face was lined with penitence.

"Annela, can you ever forgive me?" His voice wavered, and he licked his lips nervously as he continued. "I was a madman the other night. I didn't know what I was doing. It was the beer talking. I drank a bit too much with my friends and just went nuts when I thought of you and that American, so I decided to come see if you had betrayed me . . ."

"Betrayed you?" Annela croaked incredulously. "By *dancing* with someone else?"

"I know. It was stupid. But, remember what I told you the other day about those I love always breaking promises, always leaving me? I was afraid you were about to do the same thing. I'm sorry. It will never happen again." He took a step closer. With one finger he brushed a strand of hair from her face as he had so many times before, but this time he flinched and his eyes filled with pain when he noticed the slight bruise on her cheek.

"I did that," he said, then turned to the door and lowered his head. "Annela, why don't you just tell me to crawl into the sewer where I belong? I don't deserve you. Just tell me to get out of your life for good."

Annela placed a hand on his shoulder, but he didn't turn around. "Tommi, it's all right. Don't be so hard on yourself. I told you I'd always care for you, didn't I? I can't simply tell you to go away any more than I can tell my right arm to leave. What you did last night was wrong, and I won't pretend I wasn't hurt . . ." Her voice trailed off.

Tommi turned around, a glimmer of hope in his eyes. "But you'll give me another chance? A chance to prove myself to you? I need you, Annela. I need you. I love you so much, and I just can't live without you. I'll do anything."

* * *

For the next two weeks, Tommi was a girl's dream come true. Every day Annela received some kind of gift—chocolate, flowers, cards, even a necklace. He called several times a day just to say he loved and needed her desperately. When they were together, he fawned over her and gave her a flood of compliments at every turn.

Annela was beyond beautiful, he would say. Her eyes sparkled like diamonds. The tip of her nose moved when she talked—how adorable. She found herself smiling for no apparent reason, jumping up every time the phone rang, and smelling the flowers each time she walked by them.

After days of this, however, the newness started to wear off, and Annela began to wonder if Tommi really did think she had the profile of a Greek goddess, if he really did love smelling her perfume as he had said so many times that week. She felt guilty the moment such thoughts crossed her mind. After all, Tommi was simply trying to show how much he cared, how sorry he was for the night at the church, wasn't he?

By the end of the second week, any of her excitement over his attentions diminished to almost nothing. Annela came to expect the notes and cards without so much as a flutter of her heart, and his phone calls became routine. His love letters were tossed into a pile on her bedroom desk instead of being tied up with the yellow ribbon she had used for previous ones.

One night she lay awake, wondering just why she no longer swooned at the thought of him, why, now that he was again taking the discussions—his bookmark was almost at the end of Alma now—and showering her with so much attention, she didn't feel giddy or excited or . . . or in love.

Annela's eyes opened wide at the thought. That's what it came down to, she realized. She loved Tommi. She had for years. But her feelings weren't strong enough to endure beyond friendship. Deep friendship, yes, but only friendship. The realization had been coming for some time. She saw that now. Tommi's sudden gushing and her questioning of his sincerity had simply pushed it into the spotlight.

Over the next few days, she wondered how, and even if, she should tell Tommi, but she procrastinated by letting him dote on her instead. His attentions and gifts had lessened somewhat, although he still called every day to find out her schedule and say he loved her. Sister Henderson raised her right eyebrow at Annela when she didn't jump up anymore at the sound of the phone ringing. They both knew it was Tommi, and he knew her daily plans. He worked most of the time, and wouldn't be able to see her anyway. His constant calls had started to become annoying, as if she were his property, just as he had declared that night at the church. After yet another phone call, Annela hung up and found Sister Henderson sitting in her rocking chair, lips pursed, eyes drilling into her.

"What?" Annela asked, her tone defensive.

"You know what," Sister Henderson said. "You know he isn't for you, don't you? And you won't tell him. That is unfair to both of you. You *know,* but you will not act. If I recall, that's an idea you couldn't live with before, and that's why you got baptized."

"It's just that . . ."

"That what? It's easier this way? You don't want to hurt him?"

"He needs me. It would tear his heart out if we broke up now. We've been friends for so long. I don't want to lose that." Annela sat on the couch. "Besides, he needs me."

"You already said that," Sister Henderson said dryly. "It feels pretty good to be needed, doesn't it?" The rocking chair began going back and forth, back and forth, as if she were working off all the energy she had built up over the issue for the past weeks. "Dragging it out will do you no good. It can only hurt, especially when . . ." She stopped as if unsure whether she had already said too much.

"When what?"

"When he hits you again," she said bluntly. "He will, you know. They always do. Oh, they say they're sorry, and I suppose they really are. Or they think they are. But that doesn't stop them. He will hit you again, Annela. And he will come back on bended knee with flowers and sugar-coated promises. And then he will hit you again. It will go on and on, getting worse each year for the rest of your life if you let it."

Annela sat back as if someone had slapped her. It was as if her mother were talking to her through this little elderly woman. She could hear her mother's voice, see the fear in her face as Dad came toward her with the broom, see the pain in her eyes as he beat her. And then she imagined the flowers he brought home the next day.

Just like Tommi.

Except that Tommi was so sweet, so charming . . . so different on that night at the church. Could he really be a violent monster like her father? Annela could hardly believe it. The two had nothing in common. If they had, she would have shunned Tommi long ago. Wouldn't she?

But Tommi needed her. He had said so more than once. Maybe she could help him overcome it. As a friend. She had a promise to keep.

CHAPTER 9

Over the next several days, Annela couldn't stop thinking about her father and comparing him with Tommi. Then she would compare herself with her mother. She started to understand both of her parents a little better. In spite of all her father had done, she found herself wanting to clear the air with him, to at least speak with him once more.

The last Sunday of May she decided to walk home from church. It was only a few kilometers' distance, just long enough for her to sort through her emotions and decide whether to go talk to her father. When she crested the long hill leading into Roihuvuori, where both Sister Henderson's apartment and her parents' apartment lay, she knew what she had to do. Instead of turning left at the stoplight and heading toward Sister Henderson's apartment, she continued straight, crossing the street, then made her way through the familiar shops to the hill behind them. As she passed swings and climbing toys, her parents' apartment building came into view. Annela's heart beat a little quicker. She hadn't seen the long, off-white building since she had left it more than a month ago. Her jacket was probably still in the closet, she realized—unless her father had thrown it away. She wouldn't put that past him.

With a deep breath, she pulled the door open and climbed the familiar stairs. She stopped before the door with "Sveiberg" written above the mail slot. She hesitated, then knocked, even though she still had a key. Her stomach churned as she waited. A dog barked from somewhere above, and the sound sent a hollow echo vibrating through the building. When the lock clicked and the door opened a crack, Annela took a final breath of preparation. A quick gasp was followed by the door flying open. Her mother came out and all but closed the door behind her.

"Annela, what are you doing here? Is something wrong?" She glanced warily back behind her as if she could see through the door.

"I'm here to see Dad," Annela said.

"Helena, who's out there?"

"Oh, no one, just—" She turned to Annela, whispering, "Please go."

"I have to see him, Mom." Annela gave her mother a quick hug, then opened the door and walked past her through the narrow hallway and into the front room. Her father sat on his big chair, a smelly cigar stuffed between his teeth. He was shuffling through a newspaper, but when he saw her, he stopped short, and the cigar almost fell from his mouth.

"It's me, Dad. I came to apologize—"

"Get her out of here!" he snapped at Helena. With a single swift movement, his cigar was smashed into the ash tray and the newspaper thrust to the floor in a ball. He stood up and came toward Annela with his broad frame, his eyes full of rage. She took an involuntary step backward, swallowing hard.

"Dad, I—"

"Don't you *dare* call me that! I have no Mormon daughter. Now get out of here!" With each phrase he took a step forward. Annela backed up until she stood in the corridor. The door slammed shut, sending haunting echoes once more through the building. She had imagined the reunion several times all the way from the chapel, had prepared things to say and do depending on what her father did. Each version ended in a big hug, not with her standing on the other side of the door.

She hoped he wouldn't take his anger at Annela out on her mother. She leaned toward the door and listened. She heard something—maybe a kick against the wall—but no cries. She knew that her father often left for a drinking binge after his rages. Annela climbed the stairs to the next floor and sat on the top step. She would wait to see if her father came out or stayed inside to hurt her mother.

Sitting in the silence, Annela's heart wilted. She rested her face in her hands. *I shouldn't have been so blindly optimistic,* she thought. How ridiculous she had been to suppose he would even speak to her, let alone embrace her. It was silly to think her father would change. Her head came up with a sudden realization.

Tommi wouldn't change, either.

The apartment door opened, and her father stormed down the stairs. Annela stood up and breathed out heavily, resigned. She would talk to Tommi and end it once and for all.

* * *

Tommi's throat grew tight. "I knew it." He turned and began walking down the sidewalk. "One more betrayal to add to my collection."

Annela quickened her pace to catch up. "That's not fair and you know it. I'm still here for you, and I always will be. But it's just that things are changing. They *have* changed."

Tommi kept walking, his eyes fixed straight ahead, his fists balled up. *How could she say such things?* he wondered angrily. "Maybe they've changed for you. Not for me."

"Listen." Annela took his sleeve. He stopped and turned around, looking at her with watery eyes. She winced.

"Tommi, listen and believe me. The last thing I want is to lose you. I need you too. But as a *friend*, not as a boyfriend."

Tommi's heart ached. He tried to swallow but couldn't. As he spoke, his voice cracked. "You say that to make yourself feel better. But you won't call me anymore or—" He sniffed hard and looked at the ground. "Please don't say this is the end. Annela, I need you. I need you more than you'll ever know. And I love you. More than life itself. I'd die without you. Can't you see that? I can make you happy. Just tell me what to do. Anything." If it would have done any good, Tommi would have gone to his knees to plead. He waited expectantly. He had always been able to count on her. She always came around.

But Annela shook her head. She seemed to avoid looking at his face. If only she'd look at him. Then he might have a chance. She went on, staring at her hands. "You don't need to prove anything. Let me prove to you that our friendship is still important to me. I promised, didn't I?"

Her last words echoed in Tommi's mind. Yes, she had promised. But so had his mother.

* * *

Over the next two weeks Tommi was determined to win Annela back. He managed to spend several evenings with her. Once or twice he felt he was close to winning her over, and a look in her eye, a brief touch, made his hopes soar. One night they took a walk to Elephant Rock. As they sat at the edge of the water, Tommi put his arm around her shoulders. She leaned her head on it. He leaned down to kiss her, but his lips only brushed hers before she turned away and stood.

"No, Tommi."

"What is it?" he asked, his hopes dashed like the waves against the shore as he stood.

"You know what it is," Annela said. She brushed dirt from her jeans. "I'm sorry if I gave you the wrong impression . . ." Her voice trailed off when she looked at him. She took a step closer and reached out for both of his arms. "We can't go back there. You know that."

Tommi shook his head. "But I don't know it." He took a step to his backpack that lay at their feet. He unzipped the top and pulled out the Book of Mormon, handing it to her. A slip of paper stuck out halfway through. "See? I'm reading it. What else can I do?"

The bookmark slipped out and fluttered to the ground. Annela stooped to pick it up. She fingered the paper for a moment. "I'm glad you're investigating the Church, I really am."

"But?"

She smiled wanly. "But . . . things are different now."

Tommi closed his eyes and groaned. "I ruined everything that night at the church, didn't I?"

"Here's your bookmark. Where does it go?"

"Give it to me. I'll do it," he said rather brusquely, trying to grab the book.

Annela held it tighter and furrowed her brow. "Why?" She opened it. The cover cracked a little as she did. Not a single line was marked, and most of the pages still stuck together. She looked up sharply. "You haven't been reading this, have you? You've just been moving your bookmark through it, and like a fool, I believed you." She shoved it at him and pushed him out of her way.

"Annela, wait—" Tommi called after her. "I promise to start reading now. Really. It's just that I hated reading the Bible as a kid, and I figured this would be the same. I didn't realize . . ." But by that point he was talking to himself. She had left and wasn't coming back—today, at least. He looked at the blue book and threw it to the ground with a yell of frustration. His fingers clawed through his hair. Then he took a deep breath to rein in his anger. He picked up the book, brushed it off, and placed the bookmark in the front.

I'll have to read it now, he thought desperately.

* * *

"You aren't thinking about going back to him, are you?" Sister Henderson asked the next day. Annela had just hung up the phone from another apology from Tommi. "As it is, I don't approve of how often you're still seeing him."

Annela sighed and took a seat on the couch beside her. "I know. But he's had his heart broken so many times by people he loves, and I'm afraid I'll crush it all over again. I promised I'd always be his friend, but—"

"But he's not satisfied with that, is he? He's still sending you flowers in hopes that you'll change your mind."

Annela nodded. "I've had to tell him it's over every day this week. Each time he gets all upset, and I have to talk for another hour to convince him that I really mean it, and when it's all over, I end up feeling miserable, and . . ." Her voice trailed off, but Sister Henderson filled in the blank.

"And each time you get a little closer to giving in." Sister Henderson's eyebrows were raised, waiting for a response.

Annela closed her eyes and nodded. "It's almost too much. He keeps telling me how much he needs me, how much he loves me. I can't just abandon him." She added quietly, "Besides, I need him too."

"What for?"

Annela's head came up with a jolt. "What do you mean, 'what for'? He has been my friend for—"

Sister Henderson waved a knitting needle. "I know, for half your life. And I'm sure your friendship had a purpose in grade school. But what about now? Why do you need him *now*?" She stabbed the air with the needle for emphasis.

"Well, for one thing . . ." Annela fumbled for a minute, suddenly unsure of anything. She lowered her voice and admitted, "I don't know. But he loves me and *he* still needs *me*."

Sister Henderson sighed and rocked her chair. "Yes, I know it feels that way. But think about this: what would happen if you suddenly vanished from the earth? You no longer existed. What would become of him? Would he shrivel up and die?"

Annela laughed. "He says so, but of course not." She considered the question thoughtfully. "I suppose he might get even more depressed and start drinking in earnest."

Sister Henderson nodded. "All right, he might get sad and start drinking. He looks pretty miserable to me already. Can you tell me that he won't start drinking if you stay with him?"

Annela bit her tongue, unable to respond right away. Several times since *Vappu* she had smelled alcohol on Tommi's breath, even once at church, but she never said a word to him or anyone else about it. Sister Henderson had probably noticed that anyway. A few times he had said he needed to work late, but the next day he had a headache and glazed eyes. She knew he had been at parties, drinking and quite possibly doing drugs. He had admitted to being at such a party the evening of *Vappu*, and had lied about having to work.

Sister Henderson leaned in, concern written on her face. "What is it?"

"Tommi is already drinking," Annela admitted reluctantly. "He has been for a while. I hoped I could stop him." She felt her eyes stinging as she realized how ridiculous it had been to hope she could change him, to believe he really cared at all about the Church.

"Tommi is already starting to pull you down, and you can't pull him up if he doesn't want to come with you. You have to cut it off completely, Annela, for your own sake."

"I don't know if I can," she said honestly.

Sister Henderson shook her head and smiled softly as if reminding a schoolgirl of a lesson already learned. "You don't have to do anything alone, anymore Annela, remember? That's what the Lord is for. He'll give you the strength. Ask for it."

"Thanks, Sister Henderson, I will." Annela stood to go into the bedroom when Sister Henderson stopped her one last time.

"A letter arrived for you today. I think it's from your mother."

Annela hurried to the end table where she found an envelope with her mother's even handwriting across the front. Inside she found a few twenty-mark bills and a little note that read only, "Annela, I think of you often, pray for you every day. I am proud that you're doing what you know is right."

Before going to bed that night, Annela put the money and the card into her purse. She knew it would take her several days to spend it. She wanted to remind her mother that she had a job now and didn't need money she couldn't afford to give, but for her sake Annela didn't dare contact her.

Annela decided to use that little card as a reminder to keep her from giving in to Tommi. If her mother had confidence that she was doing right, then she had better make sure she *was* doing right and not ending up with a man who resembled her father.

As she lay in bed, Annela thought over the past week. It had been emotionally exhausting to hold her ground. She lived with a prayer in her heart every time she saw Tommi, and it was a good thing, because he tested her resolve more each day. He pled, scolded, blamed, accused, begged for just one more kiss. She found herself wavering more than once, almost giving in. If Tommi had known just how close she had been at some moments, he would have persisted for a little longer. And yet she struggled with how to keep her promise.

But every time it was the same old thing—tragic monologues about how he couldn't live without her, martyrlike expressions when "Smoke Gets in Your Eyes" came on the radio.

Annela looked at her purse on the desk across the room and thought of her mother's note.

No more. She wouldn't return his phone calls. She would no longer arrange to see him. And she would definitely refuse any gifts.

She would not end up in her mother's shoes.

CHAPTER 10

Annela spent a few agonizing days trying to convince Tommi she would no longer see him and eventually had to simply ignore his phone calls and pray he wouldn't show up at the apartment.

One day she walked in the door from work, exhausted. She smelled the familiar aromas of Sister Henderson's legendary cooking. After depositing her shoes and jacket in the front hall, she went into the kitchen where she found Sister Henderson wearing one of the frilly aprons that were reserved for special occasions. A rutabaga sat on the counter, and a pile of carrots, another tell-tale sign—she was making two of her best casseroles.

"Good. You're home," Sister Henderson said, glancing to Annela from the carrot she was peeling. "I wanted to warn you."

"About what?"

"That I invited someone over for dinner. As I promised not to meddle in your social life without invitation to do so, I didn't want you to think I was doing it to set you up again. So if you so wish, you can escape dinner."

"Thanks. I appreciate the warning," Annela said, picking up a carrot and snapping a piece off between her teeth. "I was thinking about going to the church for the English class anyway, although you'll have to save me some food. I'd hate to miss out on it all."

From the looks of it, Sister Henderson must have been working in the kitchen for hours already. Clearly she wanted this meal to be extra special. In addition to the casseroles, Annela saw evidence of fresh salmon from the *tori,* the open-air market downtown. She had also picked up lots of fresh vegetables and fruit. Annela noticed a pot on the stove, a sweet odor wafting from it. She lifted off the lid. *Kiisseli*. Strawberry-rhubarb *kiisseli*, that delicious fruity "soup" Sister Henderson was famous for.

Annela's mouth watered. "Who did you say you invited?"

"I didn't say, but it's Elder—I mean Ken Warner. I promised to have him over, and since it's already June, I figured it was about time." Sister Henderson paused at her work and smiled wickedly.

Annela's cheeks felt hot, but she tried to sound relaxed and detached. "Kenneth Warner? He's that American visiting for the summer, right?" She munched on the carrot and wished her face would stop burning.

The corners of Sister Henderson's mouth rose. "You are welcome to stay for dinner, if you like. There'll be plenty. And I promise not to tease you once about blushing when I mentioned him."

Annela made some remark in her defense before turning and leaving. Sister Henderson's chuckle followed her out. "Can I assume the English class won't be seeing you, then?" Annela's cheeks burned again. She closed the bedroom door loudly.

"I'll take that as a yes," Sister Henderson called.

Thankfully, Sister Henderson didn't mention that Annela had changed into a dress and touched up her makeup, although she did notice, and that fact alone was embarrassing. Annela found it infuriating that she couldn't help primping.

She spent the last ten minutes before Kenneth arrived hovering about the kitchen looking helpful. When the doorbell rang, her heart jumped. Sister Henderson went to answer the door, and Annela stayed at the stove, intently poking the boiling new potatoes with a fork to assess their tenderness.

"Don't make potato soup out of those, now," Sister Henderson called over her shoulder.

"Hello, Sister Henderson." A deep voice came from the entryway. "It's so good to see this apartment again. And to smell it again."

Sister Henderson laughed as they entered the kitchen, where the small table was set for three. Annela kept herself from turning around until Kenneth addressed her.

"Hello, Annela. It's nice to see you again."

She turned around and wiped her clean hands on a dishrag. "It's nice to see you too," she said, scolding herself for noticing and smiling at the adorable cowlick over his right temple. He carried a plate with a large bowl upside down on it, which he held out to Annela.

"This is for you," he said. "I'm sorry it's not that pretty. It's my first try."

Surprised, Annela set aside her fork and took the plate. She placed it on the counter and lifted the bowl. Inside sat an obviously home-made cake with white frosting covered in chocolate crumbs. One side slumped down, as if the cake were about to tip over. Yellow frosting scrawled, "Happy Birthday, Annela" across the top.

Somewhat baffled, Annela looked up, not knowing what to say. Sister Henderson shrugged. She didn't know what Kenneth was up to, either. "Uh, thank you," Annela said. "It looks delicious. But it's . . ." She didn't know how to say it. "It's not my birthday."

Kenneth opened his mouth, but no words came out. He glanced at Sister Henderson, then back at Annela. She thought she saw his cheeks deepen a shade as he stammered, "But—I thought that—"

"My birthday is February sixth," Annela said, in an attempt at clarification.

Understanding broke over Kenneth's face, and he began to chuckle. "I saw your name and birthday on the new-member list and forgot that Americans put the numbers of dates in a different order than Europeans. So to me, 'six-two' was June second, not the sixth of February."

"Well, this looks delicious, no matter when my birthday really is. I love chocolate."

"So I hear."

Annela glanced sidelong at Sister Henderson, who blinked back innocently.

Dinner was thoroughly enjoyable. Kenneth kept up his end of the conversation, but he didn't monopolize it. He told them about his life since returning from his mission and asked Sister Henderson about hers. He inquired after several members of the ward and into Annela's life. She dodged most of those questions, unwilling to talk about her family or Tommi. Instead she turned the discussion back to him.

"I suppose your parents miss you while you are away at school," Sister Henderson said, scooping another helping of casserole onto Kenneth's plate.

He eyed the mound, seemed about to protest, then sliced a pat of butter and put it on top. "My mother has been especially lonely since my father passed away two years ago. I try to get home to Shelley to visit as often as I can."

Sister Henderson added some salt to her carrot casserole. "What about your siblings? You have three or four if I remember right. Don't they visit?"

"Sure they do. But they're all married with children. It's much easier for me to visit more often. Mom's looking forward to me finishing my doctorate next year. She has her hopes up that I'll get a job in Idaho."

"You've sure been busy," Sister Henderson said. "I didn't know you could do all that in five years."

"Graduate school usually takes longer," Kenneth admitted. "But since I don't have a family to support, I could take a heavier load and attend spring and summer terms."

Annela loved hearing Kenneth talk about Utah, where so much Church history happened, a place where the majority of people were actually members—something she could hardly comprehend. She was still toying with the idea of attending Brigham Young University to finish her own master's degree. Kenneth was in the middle of a story about climbing the "Y" when the phone rang. Annela excused herself to answer it.

"Annela, is that you?" At the sound of Tommi's voice Annela was jerked into a world she had abandoned all evening. It took her a moment to respond. "Annela?" he repeated.

She glanced into the kitchen, where Kenneth and Sister Henderson were laughing at some joke. "Yes, it's me."

"Annela, I have to see to you. Right now." Tommi's tone was lifeless. She heard his voice catch. "Annela, I need you. You have no idea—" He remained unable to speak for several seconds. She had never heard such desperation. "I can't live without you. I have to see you, right now or you might not ever see me again."

Annela repeated his words in her mind. What did he mean by saying she might never see him again? Could he be contemplating suicide? She tried not to panic or blame herself. Cutting off contact hadn't been easy, and now she questioned that decision. "Tommi, what's wrong? Where are you?"

"I have to see you. Can you come to Elephant Rock right now?"

Annela rubbed her forehead, feeling guilty for driving Tommi to such desperation. If there was ever a time to prove her friendship and keep her promise, this was it. "I'll be right there."

She hurried to the kitchen and excused herself before racing down the apartment stairs and toward the beach path, her heart beating wildly. She prayed hard the whole way, first that Tommi wouldn't do anything rash, then for wisdom to know what to say, and especially for strength. Without help, she couldn't keep her antiromance resolve in the face of a suicide attempt.

Annela raced down the beach path, her lungs burning with the effort. When she caught sight of Elephant Rock, she could barely make out Tommi's silhouette. Brush and trees stood in the way, so she couldn't tell much from his stance. He faced her direction, as if waiting for her. Annela waved to let him know it was her, and he waved back. She hurried through a small grove of trees which blocked her view of him, then rounded the brush. Tommi came into view, and Annela stopped dead in her tracks.

Tommi stood behind a picnic basket on a blanket held down at each corner by a rock. She knew without looking what was inside. He grinned. Annela had been running as fast as she could, and she tried to catch her breath, but the sight would have rendered her speechless anyway. Tommi stepped around the basket and reached out a hand as her mouth gaped open. What was going on? Her emotions switched from worry and confusion to anger.

"I hope you understand why I called," he said, with as charming a smile as she had ever seen him wear. "Trust me, I really am desperate to talk with you, to be with you. You've been a little distant lately, so I didn't know if you'd come unless I sounded real . . . persuasive."

He tried to take her hand to lead her to the blanket, but she pulled away. "What is going on?" she demanded. In response, he reached into the basket and pushed a button, sending their song floating through the air. "Tommi, no," she said, reaching for the basket to turn off the CD player.

He took her hand firmly in both of his. He cupped it tightly and kissed the top. "But why not, Annela? For old time's sake? It couldn't hurt."

She tugged at her hand, but Tommi kept his grip on it. She tried to keep her voice even in spite of the fury she felt. "I said no. That part of our relationship is over. Over. For good. I came here thinking my friend needed me, and I find out he lied just to try to win me back. And you thought that I'd be in the mood for romance?"

Tommi gazed into her eyes as if he hadn't heard a word she said. "You think I'm trying to win you back?" He chuckled and shook his head. "No. I respect your wishes. I wouldn't do that." His voice scarcely more than a whisper, he leaned closer and looked deep into her eyes. His gaze sent nothing but frustration through her body.

"Annela, my little Annela, I thought it would be nice to end our romance the right way. One last evening to remember it by." He reached out, brushed her hair aside, and stroked her cheek. His eyes were full of longing.

"One last farewell kiss." He held her chin in one hand and leaned in. She smelled alcohol on his breath and clenched her fists to keep from slapping his face as he drew near.

Annela pulled away. "Tommi, stop it."

He grabbed for both her arms and pushed her down to her knees. She couldn't move. The soft tone of his voice changed to an irritated one.

"Annela, it's not as if I'm asking that much of you. Just a farewell kiss for me to remember our love by."

She tried to free herself from his grasp, but his fingers tightened around her arms like a vise. His voice remained steady and calm, but the mask of charm evaporated. "After all, you really belong to me, and I'm setting you free. So it's simply my right to have one final night with you. I was going to be satisfied with dinner and a simple kiss, but I think I'll need quite a bit more now." He planted an iron kiss on her mouth, his grip tightening even more on her arms. His grasp hurt so much she hardly noticed the rock digging into her knees. She almost cried out in pain, but the fear coursing through her kept her silent.

Tommi gazed at her possessively, his eyes burning, no longer with longing or charm, but with something far more menacing.

Annela froze as she realized what he was thinking. She tried to squirm loose, but his grip was so tight that she feared her arm would break if she moved.

He shoved her to the ground. Her head hit a rock violently, but she didn't register pain, only horror as Tommi stood above and took off his jacket. She quickly rolled to her side and tried to stand, but he kicked her in the ribs.

"Now Annela, don't spoil the evening. It's hardly even started yet."

She made another attempt to stand. He kicked her again, this time in the stomach, and she fell to the ground, doubled up.

The fear that had consumed Annela now combined with burning anger. It no longer mattered that this was a man she had cared for. All she saw was a violent monster. When he reached for her, the stench of alcohol on his breath came over her again. Without thinking, she clawed at his eyes with fingernails. With a stunned yelp, he covered his face for a split second, long enough for her to give him a strong, swift thrust with her knee. As he gasped in surprise, she pushed him off balance, scrambled to her feet, then began running like an animal freed from a trap.

Behind her, Annela heard a faint splashing sound. He had hit the water and was scrambling back to dry rock. She didn't look back. Elephant Rock was hardly a place with many passersby, especially before swimming season, so help would not be found near.

She ran blindly through the trees, leaving the beach path in hopes that the brush would slow Tommi's drunken pursuit, or at least keep him from finding her easily. She climbed over the guardrail dividing the beach from the road and ran up the steep slope. When she reached the top, she glanced behind but didn't see Tommi. She whirled around and raced down the street. On her left she found a house with trees and bushes lining the road.

She raced up the walkway. Her knees threatened to give out with every step, and it was by sheer will that she reached the top. She pounded on the door, ringing the doorbell at the same time, then pressed her back against the side of the wooden porch and prayed that Tommi wouldn't see her through the trees before someone could open the door. Her heart pounded in her throat as she waited, near hysterics.

Footsteps sounded against the road, and Tommi yelled her name. Annela yelped at the noise and banged on the door harder. Just then it opened. Annela didn't wait to explain herself to the woman on the other side. She shoved the door open, ran inside, and shut it behind her with a bang, and it locked automatically. Once on the other side, Annela closed her eyes and evened out her breathing, which had grown ragged. Her entire body shook, and her knees felt like jelly. She opened her eyes for a moment and saw a stunned woman standing in front of her.

When Annela didn't speak, the woman took a tentative step toward her. "Can I . . . help you with something?" She was clearly foreign, speaking with an American accent, and Annela thought she looked vaguely familiar.

Suddenly Tommi banged on the door behind her. Annela backed away from it. The woman took a few steps away too, hand to her chest.

"Annela, I know you're in there." Tommi pounded a few more times. "Come out if you know what's best for you." She swallowed hard and hugged herself tightly to stop the shaking, which had now increased to the point that her teeth chattered.

"Who is that?" the woman asked. But before Annela could answer, Tommi spoke again, this time his voice laced with tenderness.

"Annela, I'm sorry. Please come out. I'm sorry, really, I am. I don't know what came over me. Please come out so I can apologize face to face. Please?" He almost sounded like a parent coaxing a child. Annela hugged the wall. "That wasn't me out there. I would never do anything to hurt you. Just let me talk to you."

She wouldn't speak to him. She couldn't. Never again. She had kept her promise to never betray him as a friend, but in return he had betrayed her in the worst way possible.

"We're calling the police," Annela yelled through the door as her rescuer dialed the number.

"Annela, don't do that," Tommi said. "Can't we talk?"

"No, we can't. And I suggest you leave before they arrive."

Tommi kicked the door hard before leaving. Annela looked at the ceiling and breathed out heavily.

"Are you all right?" the woman asked.

"I'm fine," Annela said, wondering if she dared go back home alone.

"Is he the one who came into the ward *Vappu* party?"

Only then did Annela realize that this was the mission president's wife. "He is. He doesn't take rejection well." Annela tried to smile with a shrug.

"My husband has the car today or I would give you a ride home," the sister said. "Is there someone we could call to pick you up?"

Annela gratefully sat on a chair next to the phone and dialed Sister Henderson's number. The mission president's wife sat on the chair that flanked the other side. Sister Henderson wouldn't be much protection, but she would be able to send someone who was. With a jolt of embarrassment, Annela realized it would most likely be Kenneth. He was undoubtedly still there, and Sister Henderson would send him. Annela hated the idea of him rescuing her from this kind of situation. Annela chose her words carefully.

"Hi. It's me," she said. "I have a slight problem here. Tommi—he—I'm at the mission home right now. Could you send someone to get me? He might be waiting outside, and I'd rather not come home alone." That was enough detail for now, Annela thought. Sister Henderson could get a greater explanation later if she demanded it. Annela couldn't get herself to say what Tommi had tried to do. Not yet. And not over the phone.

Sister Henderson's normally gentle voice was tense. *"What happened,* Annela? What did he do?"

"I'm fine," she said.

"Did he strike you?"

"Yes," Annela admitted reluctantly.

"Did he draw blood?"

"I'm not bleeding," Annela assured her, but then remembered her head. She reached up and touched a warm patch of blood at the back. The mission president's wife gasped and ran to her kitchen.

"I'm fine, Sister Henderson," Annela said again. "I just don't think it's the best idea for me to leave alone, that's all."

"Ken will be right there. And you're going to tell me all about this when you get here." It was a statement, not a request.

The mission president's wife returned with a damp cloth, which she pressed against Annela's cut. By the time Kenneth arrived a few minutes later, the bleeding had almost stopped. He escorted her back to the apartment in the used VW bug he had bought for the summer. He didn't pry into what had happened beyond asking about the wound on the back of her head.

"Does it hurt?"

"Not much," she said.

He glanced over from the steering wheel. "When I walked up, I saw someone in a blue coat dash around the corner. Tommi?"

She nodded. "Probably."

"Then it was smart to have someone come for you."

Kenneth didn't force any more conversation on her, for which she was grateful. Her hands shook the whole way, even though she clasped them together. As she stared out of the car window and watched pine trees and buildings go by, her eyes burned. Tears wouldn't come yet, although they would eventually, she knew.

* * *

Once Annela was safely inside, Kenneth asked if he could be of any more help. For once Sister Henderson paid little attention to him. She headed for the kitchen where she moistened an old dishrag for Annela's wound.

"Thank you for bringing her back," Sister Henderson said, dabbing at the back of Annela's head. "But I think we'll be all right. Thanks for coming to dinner. We'll see you at church on Sunday."

"Are you sure the two of you will be safe alone?" he asked.

Sister Henderson nodded. "We'll be fine." She felt a twinge of guilt for not being the perfect hostess, but Annela needed her more than Ken did at the moment.

He thanked her for the meal and quietly excused himself. Sister Henderson led Annela into the living room to finish nursing the cut. It turned out to be very small, but Annela would have a nice bump on the back of her head for a while. She worked for a minute without saying anything, her mind playing out possible scenarios of what happened at the beach, each one worse than the previous.

"Press this against it," she said, giving Annela the dishcloth. Then Sister Henderson closed her eyes, clasped her hands, and took a deep breath.

"Annela," she said, "what did he do to you?"

Annela's voice caught. "Nothing actually happened."

"But did he try to . . ." Sister Henderson couldn't say the word.

Annela nodded reluctantly. "But I got away before he could."

Sister Henderson looked down at her hands and nodded. "Good." She said nothing for a few moments, but then had to ask the next question on her mind. "Are you still going to 'be there' for him?" Her tone was angry.

A sob crept up Annela's throat and escaped. She just shook her head, and her free hand flew to her face. "I can't," she croaked. "I can't ever see him again."

"Good," Sister Henderson said again. Her heart ached for Annela. But keeping Tommi out of her life would make her happier in the long run, so Sister Henderson was relieved to hear that Annela had made the right decision.

She patted Annela's hand and pursed her lips in thought. "Good," she said once more. There really wasn't anything else to say.

"What can I do now?" Annela said between choked sobs. "I feel so guilty, as if I were the one who did something wrong."

"Nonsense."

"I can't help but think of what could have happened, and how I could have prevented it altogether by listening to you in the first place. Look what I almost got myself into." She bit her lips until they almost bled. She wiped at her cheeks. "What can I do now? He won't stay away. I know that now. He'll always keep trying to come back."

Sister Henderson nodded her head in silent agreement.

"I'm scared. I keep picturing him saying I've betrayed him, even though I know better, that I can't be around him anymore."

Sister Henderson sat silently, letting Annela toss her thoughts out as she sorted through the jumbled mess. The sooner Annela could work through them, the better, the older woman reasoned. Annela's emotions were gradually coming under control now, but she still poured out her thoughts and feelings.

"I've been counting on Tommi getting baptized so we could marry. It seemed so . . . convenient, I guess. Better than any of my other prospects in Finland, anyway." Annela stopped as a realization seemed to hit her. She turned to look at Sister Henderson, her red eyes tinged with a new sadness. "There's no one here for me, is there?"

Sister Henderson's heart sank at the sight of Annela facing this new discovery about herself. She tried to hug away the hurt in Annela's eyes. "I don't know."

CHAPTER 11

Over the next week, everything became mechanical for Annela—waking up, eating, going to work, coming home. Her scriptures and prayers were the only things keeping her sane, and she depended on them as she never had. Only a few parts stood out in the blur of each passing day—the 3 A.M. bouts of crying, Tommi's phone calls or hang-ups if Sister Henderson answered, and Annela's jumpiness at work each time she saw a young man with blond hair or a blue coat. And as the majority of Finnish men were blond, she found herself always on edge. What would she say to Tommi if he came by? What would he do? As irrational as she knew it was, Annela feared he would come after her at The Candy Bag.

Sometimes, as she rang up customers, she composed speeches—some brilliantly caustic—that she could use if the opportunity ever arose, though she knew she would never really use them. At church Kenneth tried to speak with her and asked if he could help in any way. But she responded coolly. Her emotions were still too raw for her to rely on a male for comfort. She was grateful for his friendly concern, even if she never showed it.

One day at work Annela saw someone familiar pass one side of the store. With her eyes, Annela followed the girl along the other side of the store as she turned the corner. She realized it was Kirsti, walking with some friends Annela had never seen before. Her little sister looked so different that she wasn't sure at first that it really was Kirsti. She had dyed her hair a dark reddish, almost purple color and wore tight jean cut-offs—about as short as they could be. Her tank top was cropped and tight. Her friends had a variety of hair colors among them. Some wore leather and carried beer bottles. Others sported odd piercings and black eyeliner. Annela thrust a receipt at a customer.

"Mia, cover for me," she said and ran out without waiting for a response. "Kirsti!" she yelled. Several shoppers stopped and looked around, including her sister, unsure of where the voice was coming from. When Kirsti looked over, her face went through several expressions, initial surprise followed by joy, embarrassment, and finally, disgust. Annela decided that Kirsti's original smile expressed her real feelings, and the tough face she put on last was a mask for the benefit of her new buddies.

"Kirsti! It's been forever since I've seen you," she said, crushing her sister in a hug, something they never did at home. Kirsti reeked of cigarette smoke.

The act took Kirsti back a step, and she looked at Annela suspiciously. "What are you doing here?"

"I work here," Annela said, motioning toward the shop as if her brown-and-orange-striped apron with "The Candy Bag" written across it didn't give it away. "What are you doing?"

"Just hanging out."

Annela glanced at Kirsti's hair, her clothes, her friends, and tried to imagine their father's reaction to her new look. "How are you doing?"

"Fine."

"And how is everything at home?" Annela asked in hopes of getting some inkling of how their mother was doing.

"Fine."

The small talk was probably irritating her, Annela realized, but she didn't want to let Kirsti go. Not yet. She racked her mind for a topic, and realized that it was the summer break now. "How did you do in school?"

"Fine."

"And Mom? How is she?"

"Fine."

Annela knew she wouldn't be getting any information, at least not as long as her buddies were around, so she let her sister go. "Tell everyone I'm fine too. Come see me at work sometime, all right? I work most days."

"Sure. See ya later," Kirsti said, heading off toward the escalators. Annela watched Kirsti walk away and descend the escalator, then she returned to her station at the store. Her thoughts went back to Kirsti off and on for the rest of the day, and Annela worried about her little sister, hoping she was all right. She sure didn't look it. Their father must have been livid the first time he smelled smoke on her breath—he must have noticed by now. And what had his reaction been to her hair?

But then Annela realized that he might not have cared at all. Kirsti was his angel, his favorite, and his only other child was "dead." What did it matter if she dyed her hair or took up smoking? If only Annela could have really talked with her to find out how their mom was doing.

Deep in thought, Annela mechanically asked what she could do for the next customer.

"Could I get half a kilo of Turkish Peppers?" came a voice with an American accent.

Annela looked up, and her heart jumped into her throat. "Hello, Kenneth. I didn't notice you coming in."

Kenneth gave a crooked smile and shrugged. "Just had a craving for Turkish Peppers. But now that I'm here . . ."

"A half kilo, did you say?" she broke in, unwilling to give him the opportunity to pry. Kenneth nodded to confirm the amount, and Annela set to weighing the hard, black candy. "Half a kilo is quite a lot. It's rare to find a foreigner who likes Turkish Peppers. They're too strong even for many Finns." She eyed the scales to avoid Kenneth's gaze.

"I haven't had any for a long time," Kenneth said. "You should have seen my face the first time I tried one. I had been out of the MTC for about a month when my companion gave me one. He told me to bite into it. I didn't know about the hot powder inside, but then . . ." He chuckled at the memory. "My face felt ready to explode. I must have cried for ten minutes. But now I can't get enough of them."

Annela rang up the candy and handed the striped paper bag across the counter to Kenneth. "There you go. Have a good day."

"Thanks." Kenneth turned to go, but stopped before the next customer could step forward. "Annela?" He licked his lips and tried again, his face now darkening several shades. "Would you spend

Juhannus with me? During my mission I always heard how wonderful Seurasaari was, but I never got the chance to go. Would you show me around?"

A rejection hung about her lips, but then she reconsidered. *Juhannus* would be awful if she stayed home and had nothing to do but remember last year's holiday with Tommi. "Sure. I'd love to."

He smiled broadly, then popped one of the candies into his mouth and bit it hard. "Great! How's seven o'clock? We'll do dinner, too."

Annela nodded. With that, he left the store and headed toward the escalators.

She stared after him and wondered if she would regret the decision. *How will it be to spend Juhannus without Tommi? At Seurasaari, no less.* She wouldn't be able to take Kenneth to see the stilts. But then, she couldn't imagine Kenneth even wanting to try them. He didn't strike her as the type who needed attention to have fun.

"Excuse me. *Excuse me.*"

Annela shook her head and returned to the present, where a young woman with tight jeans and big hair waited to be served.

* * *

As luck would have it, Kenneth's car broke down the day before *Juhannus*, so they took the bus and the metro on their date. While they sat on the metro, Kenneth apologized again for the inconvenience, and Annela had to convince him that she really didn't mind.

"I grew up without a car," she reminded him. "I'm used to public transportation."

"I forget," Kenneth said with a laugh. "Back home you almost have to own a car to get around."

They lapsed into silence for a moment, the humming metro the only sound. Kenneth gazed out the window. "I've always loved the Helsinki skyline," he said. "You forget about some things until you see them again."

Annela's gaze shifted to the window and she saw what he meant. The dark shapes of buildings rising from the ground against the royal blue sky were impressive. She hadn't noticed the view for years, if ever. Not really noticed, anyway.

Turning to her, Kenneth said, "It's been so long since I left Finland that I don't remember where many things are anymore. You'll have to pick where we eat and show me how to get there."

"All right, what sounds good to you?" she asked. "There's an American pizza restaurant downtown, a block or so from the train station."

"No, I'm only here for the summer, so I want something I can only get here—although I can pass on liver casserole." Kenneth grimaced and shuddered as he remembered the dish.

"That bad?"

"You have no idea. I had two companions who couldn't get enough of it, so we had it at dinner appointments all the time. The smell alone nearly did me in by the time I went home."

"I never did care for it much, either, although I had to choke it down as a kid at school lunch." An idea occurred to her. "So you want something you can get only here? Then let's not go to a restaurant at all." Kenneth looked back with confused eyes. She laughed. "We'll stop at a meat pie stand, then maybe find a bread or pastry shop for some *pulla*. Can't get much more Finnish than that, can you?"

"That really sounds good right now. I've missed those pies."

They took their time walking through the streets of Helsinki as they looked for a vendor. It didn't take too long to find one. "How many do you want?" Kenneth asked.

Annela held up a finger. "Oh, one is fine. But with lots of mustard."

Kenneth ordered two for himself. "It's been so long," he said as if he had to explain himself. He handed Annela the scone with meat and rice filling. "Here you go. One with lots of mustard."

Kenneth took his pies, one in each hand, but when he tried to take a bite out of one, the ketchup, mustard, and all the fillings started oozing out. As he had no free hand, his hand and face were soon covered. His eyes flew open.

"Oh, that's hot," he said, now gripping both pies in his left hand so he could shake the filling from his right. More filling dripped onto the sidewalk before Annela managed to take the pastries and free his hands. He began salvage efforts to clean up the mess.

"Are you all right?" Annela asked, trying not to smile too broadly.

"Oh, I'm fine," Kenneth said with a chuckle. "Just forgot how to eat these, that's all."

Kenneth managed to finish his meat pies without further mishap. He tossed the tissues into the trash, then looked around. "I don't see any bakeries nearby. Let's go for ice cream instead. Let me know if you see an ice cream stand or a soda machine."

"Agreed."

As they walked on, Annela eyed him from the side, thinking it was fun to be around someone rediscovering her country, seeing things in a fresh new way. She started to see things differently too, just being around him. Like when Kenneth mentioned how much he loved cobblestone streets. There weren't too many left in Helsinki, but Kenneth talked as if all streets should be made that way.

"They're more durable than any asphalt made today, and they're so beautiful. Although," he said remembering his mission, "they're murder to ride a bike on in the rain." He wanted to make sure they took a walk along a cobblestone street before the summer was over.

They soon found an ice-cream stand and each chose a cone of chocolate- and nut-covered ice cream. Soon after, Kenneth spotted a pop machine and bought two bottles of M.A.C. Black Orange soda. "This is my favorite drink of all time." Kenneth downed half of his bottle, then smacked his lips with pure satisfaction.

"Is it as good as you remembered?" Annela asked.

"Better. And different. There's just something about being here and being able to walk around—see all the sights I want to—without having to worry about my next appointment or my companion. It's a bit odd, actually. Even though I've been off my mission for over five years, I still feel as if I'm breaking some rule by being alone with you."

"I'm sorry."

"Don't apologize. I'm enjoying myself thoroughly."

They reached the white bridge that led across the small waterway to Seurasaari. Halfway across, Kenneth stopped and went to the side where a cluster of ducks swam below, hoping for crumbs from people passing above. Annela joined him at the edge as he breathed in the cool summer air.

"It's as beautiful as I heard," he said. Then just as suddenly, "All right. Let's go."

They wandered along the wide dirt paths to the exhibits, first to the old boats which were on display year-round, then to the exhibits out for the holiday, like the women in traditional costumes who carded and spun flax. At the edges of the island they could see the bonfires floating in the water as part of the holiday.

Soon they came to a large wooden platform where costumed performers did national dances. Annela tried to explain as best as she could remember some of the differences in the costumes; various parts of the country were represented by colors, styles of headdress, and the design on the pocket that hung from the waist.

They headed down the paths again. Annela began playing with a small stick—twisting off the leaves and peeling bark away to reveal tender green skin beneath the dry, rough outside. "I wish I remembered more about the costumes," she said. "I should have paid more attention in school when we learned about them. I don't even know most of the stories of the *Kalevala*—just a handful, like the ones painted on the ceiling of the National Museum. I've always loved history, but I've studied other countries' histories more than my own. Pretty sad."

"Not really," Kenneth said. "I've been fascinated by history and other cultures all of my life, but I'd be willing to wager that you know more about American history than I do. I could tell you about every English monarch since William the Conqueror, but I can't name the first ten U.S. presidents."

"So we're both pretty sad," Annela said with a wry grin.

Kenneth gave her a playful smile. "I think we're two scholars of a different breed, that's all. Good thing we found each other."

Annela tossed the stick aside with a laugh and wiped her hands together to get the flecks of bark off them. When she looked up, the two of them were entering the open amphitheater where the stilts lay. She could envision Tommi teetering on one pair, singing loudly as tourists stared. She stopped short, and her throat tightened. Kenneth walked on for a few steps before realizing she was no longer beside him. He turned around.

"There you are," he said, coming back.

Seeing the stilts gripped her, an emotion she was completely unprepared for. Her hand involuntarily went to her cheek, almost feeling the sting from Tommi's first strike at the church, seeing his eyes as he crawled toward her at Elephant Rock.

"Annela, are you all right?" Kenneth rushed over. "What is it?"

She shook her head and tried to think. "It's nothing. I—it's just—it's nothing."

"Do you want to sit down?"

"No, really. I'm fine."

In spite of her protestations, Kenneth led her to a bench at the edge of the trees. Annela knew he had no idea he had just made the problem worse by entering the very location that first sent her heart beating. But if she protested, she would have to explain, and she refused to bring up Tommi tonight. Kenneth sat beside her and took one of her hands. The touch also took her off guard, sending a thrill up her arm.

"Look how pale you are," he said, looking at her hand. Annela's heart quickened. There was no way her face was pale any longer.

"I'm always pale," Annela said, trying to lighten the mood. "Sister Henderson says I could have been mistaken for a ghost in my baptismal dress."

Kenneth laughed softly. "Are you all right? What's wrong?"

Annela forced a smile. "It's nothing. I'm fine."

But despite her assurance, Kenneth didn't release her hand. Instead he interlocked their fingers and held on securely. A part of Annela cried out betrayal at holding one man's hand in a place packed with so much emotion related to another. But the rest of her had no desire to pull away. She was content to sit on the bench, her hand in Kenneth's large, warm one, as the thrills kept shooting up her arm.

He stood, holding her hand. "Ready to go?"

She nodded. *This is crazy*, she kept telling herself as they made their way down the dirt path again. *So he's holding my hand. It shouldn't feel like such a big deal, should it? But it is. Why am I reacting like this?* She kept eyeing her hand to see if it really was in Kenneth's.

Annela figured he must have taken her hand out of sympathy, or perhaps out of worry. It was for support, she decided. She had read a whole lot into nothing. In the end she decided to simply enjoy herself, whatever Kenneth's motives were.

CHAPTER 12

Annela ate lunch with Mia again the following week. Instead of going to Clock's, she brought Mia to the food window on the Hansa Bridge, both to convert her to their french fries and to see if her body did in fact evaporate fat on contact. Mia looked great as usual, but this time Annela didn't envy her. Instead she looked forward to a good lighthearted chat. When they got their orders and were seated on the plastic white chairs, Annela expected Mia to plunge into chatter about her latest hair or boy crisis, but she was quieter than usual. Annela filled in the silence by telling Mia about her date with Kenneth.

"Sister Henderson promised not to meddle, and she didn't," Annela said. Truth be told, Annela felt pretty sure that, after her weak-kneed episode, Kenneth pitied more than liked her. She doubted that holding her hand had the same effect on him that it had on her. And that fact cut a bit.

"But then, Sister Henderson didn't need to meddle. I'm sure she could tell just by looking at me that it went well. Oh, and get this. As she made breakfast, she hummed 'I Love to See the Temple.' I'm sure I blushed berry red, I was so embarrassed. We've only been on a single date. It's not as if he's even thinking about the temple at this point, right?"

Mia looked up with a confused look on her face. "What's the temple?"

Annela flushed just like she had at breakfast. She realized that Mia didn't know what that meant, and actually saying it was hard. "That's where members of our church get married."

"Oh." Mia nodded and gave Annela a wan smile. "Well, I'm glad you had fun. He sounds nice." Her gaze drifted to the escalators.

Annela's eyebrows knit together. Mia definitely wasn't her usual self today if she had no interest in discussing men. "What's the matter? You seem distant."

"I'm just thinking."

"About what?" Annela asked.

Mia tossed a fry to the table. She eyed Annela and demanded, "Why are you so beautiful?"

Annela burst out laughing and caught some rude glares from several passing shoppers. She instantly put her hands to her mouth to stop the noise. "You have got to be kidding. Look at yourself, Mia, and then look at me. I'm not ugly, exactly, but—just—well, look at you. You're *gorgeous*."

Mia tucked one of her shiny dark locks behind her ear and shook her head. "That's not what I mean. There's something that hangs about you. Or maybe it's in your eyes. I don't know. You're all lit up inside, and not because of makeup or anything. It's something I want and don't have."

Annela paused, digesting what Mia had said and remembering their previous conversation. "Is it the thing you're looking for?"

"I don't know." Mia sat back in her chair with folded arms. "I've almost given up looking."

Annela thought carefully before responding. One wrong word, and she might push Mia away. "I think I know what you're talking about. What you're seeing in me is the . . ." Annela coughed slightly and finally managed to say the words. "It's the Holy Ghost."

Mia's eyebrows went up. "Like in the Bible?"

Annela breathed out deeply. Now that the awkward beginning of the topic was past, she plunged in. "That's right. It's the *gift* of the Holy Ghost. It's something I was given after I was baptized. It's part of what I told you about before."

Mia smiled ruefully and looked away. "Thanks, Annela. I appreciate the effort, but as I told you before, I'm not much of a religious person." Somewhat under her breath she added, "If only the answer could be so easy."

It can. It is. Annela longed to say the words, but knew the time wasn't right. Mia wasn't ready to have someone's testimony thrust upon her. After a few awkward moments of silence, Mia abandoned her forlorn expression and replaced it with her bubbly one as quickly as if she had removed one mask and donned another. She went on to debate shades of nail polish and whether one would look good with a French manicure. Annela went along with the charade until they went back to work.

The rest of the day Mia seemed distracted, but although she didn't bring up their conversation, the yearning look returned whenever she took a break from weighing candy and ringing up orders. The sight sent Annela's stomach twisting in frustrated knots, and it was all she could do to keep from spilling her testimony out to Mia on the spot. Once again Annela didn't pay attention to the next person in line, and was stunned to look up and see her mother standing there with a sheepish look on her face.

"Mom!" It came out as a squeal. Annela asked Mia if she could run the counter alone for a few minutes, then hurried her mother into the back room. She finally got to take a look at her mother for the first time in too long.

Annela's mother had her thin blond hair pulled back, and she wore a long-sleeved navy shirt and worn-out jeans. Annela wasn't sure, but she thought they were an old pair she had left behind. If her father had realized they were his daughter's he wouldn't have let his wife wear them. He obviously hadn't paid much attention to his daughter's wardrobe.

Her mother's tired eyes belied her smile. Annela pulled up an old stool from the corner. "Have a seat."

She sat with a sigh of fatigue. "It's good to see you, Annela, even if it's only for a few minutes." She eyed the clock on the wall.

"How much time do you have?" Annela asked, noting the time too.

"I'll have to leave in five minutes or so. Kirsti is trying on some shoes and doesn't know I'm here. I'm supposed to meet her by the sunglasses at Pukeva at a quarter after."

Annela sat across from her mother on an empty crate. Neither of them spoke for a moment, although they both had much to say and simply didn't know where to begin. "Dad didn't hurt you after I came by the other day, did he?"

Annela's mother shook her head. "No."

Annela raised her eyebrows. "Mom . . ."

"I promise," she said. "He didn't touch me. He yelled a bit, and the front room lamp no longer exists, but other than that, no harm done."

At the mention of her father, Annela decided to ask a question that had been haunting her. She kept her voice even, holding back the emotion the question brought up. "Why does Dad hate me?"

"He doesn't—"

But Annela cut her off. "It's no use denying it. I know he does. It's more than plain anger. He actually despises his own daughter." Her eyes grew teary as she voiced the thoughts that had been with her for so long.

Her mother stared at the floor. Then she blinked, and a tear rolled down one cheek. She closed her eyes and bit her lips together before saying, "There are a lot of things you do not know about and can't understand, Annela. It is not you that he despises. It is what he sees in you."

"I don't understand . . ." Annela's voice trailed off, hoping her mother would step in and explain. Instead her mother looked up with intense eyes and shook her head.

"I can't talk about it. Maybe someday I'll be ready to." She clasped her hands together and stared at them. "Dad has done a lot of bad things, Annela. I'll be the first to admit that. But he isn't the only one who has made mistakes. We all need to forgive."

"You're a lot better than I would be in your place," Annela said bitterly. "I don't know if I'll ever be able to forgive him."

Her mother placed a hand over Annela's. "He has had a hard life. Don't judge him. You don't know the whole story. But I want you to remember one thing. Even when it didn't seem like it, *I* always loved you." Her eyes grew misty, and she reached out a hand to cradle Annela's face. "When you were a little girl, I always knew when you were crying, and my arms ached to hold you."

Annela's lips trembled, and she found herself in a longed-for embrace. Her mother's arms nearly crushed her, as if making up for all the years they never hugged. When they finally pulled away from each other, both of their cheeks sparkled with wetness.

"Here, take this," her mother said after wiping at her cheeks. She placed a crumpled bill in Annela's hand. A hundred-mark bill.

Annela tried to give it back. "I don't need your money now that I have a job. You can't afford to give it to me. Dad will find out."

But her mother would have none of it. "I have to go now," she said, dodging the money. She headed toward the door. "I'll try to come visit as often as I can."

Annela stepped forward as her hand rested on the door handle. "I'd love to see you as often as you can make it. But Mom, promise me you won't come if it means getting Dad mad. I would rather not see you at all than know you're hurt."

"Annela, you worry too much. I'll be fine."

"Mom, promise."

"Who's the mother here?" she said in mock protest. "All right, I promise." She let go of the door handle and wrapped her arms around Annela again. "I'll be praying for you," she whispered before opening the door and walking away.

CHAPTER 13

The following week Annela took Kenneth to the National Museum, which she hadn't been to in at least ten years. They stopped on the second-floor balcony and looked at the four *Kalevala* paintings depicted on the domed ceiling.

"They say that the American author Longfellow lifted the idea for *Hiawatha* from the *Kalevala*," Kenneth told her. "There was quite a scandal. Some people even accused him of plagiarism."

"I had no idea our national stories reached so far," Annela said. She looked at the ceiling and shivered. "I've always hated that one," she said, pointing to a picture of a man plowing through snakes.

"It's not the most beautiful of the *Kalevala* paintings, is it?" Kenneth said. "I've always thought one of the best ones is where Aino escapes from Väinämöinen. Such a sad story, for both of them."

Annela agreed it was sad, although she had always sided with Aino, the beautiful maid who was expected to marry the old man Väinämöinen. Horrified, she ran away from him and drowned herself. In typical mythology fashion, Aino turned into a fish. Later, when Väinämöinen was fishing, he caught her, but she escaped. The painting depicted the human form of Aino escaping his hands back into the water. Annela never pitied Väinämöinen.

"Come on," Kenneth said, taking her hand and dragging her out. "Let's get some lunch." Annela gently extracted her hand from Kenneth's, hoping he didn't notice. *Juhannus* was the only time she had let him keep it. Ever since, she recoiled each time he touched her as if he were Tommi. To her relief, today Kenneth didn't seem to notice. He stopped on their way out to buy a few postcards from the museum, including one with the painting of Aino and Väinämöinen. "Just a little memento," he told Annela as he gave the cards to her.

* * *

Later that week they took the ferry to Helsinki's island zoo. One area had small glass cases in the walls. Annela and Kenneth walked along, reading information cards and such until Kenneth stopped and laughed out loud.

"Look at this," he said, pointing. Annela leaned over to examine a tiny exhibit of a cricket. "I doubt you could find anyone willing to actually pay to see one of those in Utah. They're everywhere. I never thought I'd see a cricket in a zoo."

They walked along paths on the outskirts of the island and talked about their childhoods. When they found a shady spot, they set up a picnic and Kenneth paused in his recollection about growing up in Idaho as he unloaded their lunch from his bag.

"I don't suppose you ever imagined yourself coming to Finland on your mission, let alone studying its literature for graduate school," Annela said. She had heard several missionaries say that they had to look at a map to even find the country when they got their calls. One admitted to looking in Asia instead of Europe and being relieved to discover that Finland wasn't a third-world country.

Kenneth opened a plastic bag of raspberries. "Actually, it wasn't a surprise. And that's the strange part."

Annela reached into the bag. "Why is that?" she asked, curious.

"Because of my great-grandfather. He worked in the Scofield Mine down in central Utah. There was a massive explosion—it's considered the worst mine disaster in U.S. history—and my great-grandfather was rescued by a Finnish immigrant. Ever since, my family has felt a connection with Finland, sort of an admiration and a debt to the Finns. So it seemed fitting that I got to come here on my mission."

Annela's hand had stopped midair, a raspberry centimeters from her mouth. "I know about that mine disaster."

"You do? How? It was over a century ago in a tiny city in the middle of nowhere."

"True. But a lot of Finns immigrated there—most of the deaths from the explosion were Finns, if I remember right. My great-grandfather went in search of making his fortune. After the disaster he came back home."

Kenneth shook his head and unwrapped a sandwich. "Wow. Small world."

"The family story says he saved a man's life in the disaster," Annela said, staring at Kenneth.

Kenneth's head came up sharply. "What was his name?"

"Matti Heikilä. The man he rescued was named George."

Kenneth's jaw hung open slightly. His cheeks pulled back into a smile as he shook his head in disbelief. "My great-grandfather's name was George. It's almost as if . . ." His voice trailed off, and he left the sentence unfinished, but his cheeks colored. "Here you go," he said as he held out the sandwich.

Annela took it, and their hands touched for a moment. She caught her breath, but then pulled away, wishing she didn't have the recurring gut reaction of fear each time he touched her. She wondered if Matti Heikilä were watching them from somewhere beyond, berating her for pushing away the descendant of the man he had saved.

Saved for her? The thought jumped into her mind before she could stop it.

* * *

Kenneth quickly adopted the habit of taking Annela and Sister Henderson to and from church every week, and Sister Henderson made him dinner afterward. He would then stay and talk, and sometimes he played the old piano in the living room. He and Annela read books aloud, sometimes from Sister Henderson's complete collection of Agatha Christie novels, while Sister Henderson sat knitting in her rocking chair. With summer nights remaining light well past bedtime, Kenneth easily stayed late without anyone realizing what time it was until someone yawned and looked at the clock.

It was a relief that Annela hadn't talked to Tommi in weeks. She no longer answered the phone, although that didn't stop him from

leaving nasty messages. Once or twice she had seen him in the neigh-
borhood, and she had received a few threatening letters mentioning
Kenneth's visits, so Annela knew Tommi had been watching the
apartment. But his influence hung on in other ways—she still shrank
from Kenneth's touch.

Intellectually she knew her actions were silly, that Kenneth was
nothing but a gentleman and everything Tommi wasn't. And at first
she didn't feel bad about it. After all, she was convinced she cared
more for Kenneth than he did for her. But as they spent more time
together, she could see the hurt in his eyes when she recoiled, like the
day they went to the Sibelius monument in late July.

They had climbed the rocks under the large organ-style metal
pipes. When her foot slipped, Kenneth steadied her. As soon as she
regained her footing, her throat constricted with the same sick
feeling, and she tried to slip her fingers away.

Kenneth held on tighter, and she had to stop and look at him. As
usual, he didn't say a word, but she could see the hurt in his eyes
when she reclaimed her hand and said merely, "Thanks." She sought
refuge by taking several strides farther and then looking up,
pretending to be engrossed in the pipes and the pale blue sky visible
through them. Kenneth didn't follow for a minute, and out of the
corner of her eye, Annela was acutely aware of him looking at the
ground, hands in his pockets.

I'm sorry, Annela thought to herself. *I'm so sorry.* But she couldn't
get her mouth to form the words.

* * *

It was a week or so later when she and Kenneth boarded the ferry
for the twenty-minute ride to the old island fortress called
Suomenlinna, the Castle of Finland, once used to protect Helsinki
from sea invasion. Although it was now a tourist attraction, some
retired military men lived in renovated and modernized apartments
within the fortress.

Ever since Annela's third-grade class visited it, she had loved
wandering around the island, although she hadn't been back in several
years. She loved the thick stone walls, which could surely hold out

anything. They had openings that were wide on one end and narrow on the other so soldiers could see out and fire their guns without the enemy being able to see them. She felt safe and protected inside it and imagined that's what a real home felt like.

As the ferry cut a wake through the water, Annela didn't watch the island. Instead she leaned her back against the railing and watched the Helsinki skyline recede.

"It really is beautiful, isn't it?" she said. "I'm glad you pointed it out to me."

Kenneth joined her at the rail and nodded. "I didn't realize how much I missed it." He reached over and laid a hand on hers.

She withdrew it, then turned around and looked at the island. "I haven't been to the fortress since I was ten. Or twelve, maybe," she said, trying a little too hard to sound casual and ignore the hurt and frustrated expression on Kenneth's face. He didn't answer. Instead he sighed, his jaw working intently. The silence grew tense, and Annela tried to think of something to say.

"Sister Henderson tells me you're going to accept a job offer," she said.

Kenneth sighed and seemed to agree to the change in topic. "That's right. At BYU—Idaho. My mom really wants me to take it. It would bring me closer to home. She's been lonely since my dad passed away."

"When would you start?"

"As soon as I get back, fall semester. It would be a year contract with the possibility of a renewal."

"What about finishing your degree?"

Kenneth shrugged. "My class work is done. I just have my dissertation to finish, and I can do most of that from Rexburg with e-mail and occasional trips to Provo." He didn't sound all that excited about the prospect.

"Do you *want* to take the job?"

Kenneth considered. "I've already accepted it. They were really in a bind. Since they lost a teacher to a sudden illness, they had to fill the position quickly. I suppose it'll be a good experience."

Their silence returned, and things remained a little strained until the ferry docked. Annela showed Kenneth all her favorite spots in the fortress, including the spot where her camera was stolen one summer. After an hour, Kenneth seemed fine, but she still felt guilty. It wasn't fair to him now that he clearly saw her as more than a friend. When they boarded the return ferry, Annela went to the rail instead of finding a seat inside. Kenneth was in much better spirits, and chatted jovially about his family. Annela eyed his hand, only centimeters from her own, and gulped. Kenneth's voice faded into the background as she got up the courage to leap over the hideous fears that bound her. With a deep breath, she inched her hand over and put it on top of his.

"So I told my mom—" Kenneth stopped cold and looked down at their hands, then at Annela. She gave him a wan smile, her heart racing with nervousness as she waited for his reaction. He turned his hand over to enclose hers, stroked it with his thumb, and smiled back. "So I told her that I really am a grown man and can do my own laundry," he finished quietly.

She had heard only half of the story, but doubted that Kenneth would have cared either way. The rest of the ferry ride was spent in a warm silence, hand in hand as they watched the wake ripple out behind them.

When Kenneth brought her back to the apartment, he smiled, squeezed her hand again, and said, "Thanks for showing me around today."

"My pleasure."

"Oh, I forgot something." Kenneth reached into his inner jacket pocket and produced a small package. "It's just something little. When I saw it in the store, I thought of you."

"Thanks," she said.

"You can open it inside," he said, putting it into her hands.

She nodded, still looking at the silver wrapping paper and pink ribbon. Kenneth coughed slightly and said, "Oh. And one more thing."

"What's that?" she asked, looking up.

Kenneth leaned in, and she caught a whiff of his cologne. A flutter of butterflies went through her, but before he could kiss her, the familiar fear gripped her again. She ducked and fumbled in her purse in search of her keys.

Kenneth pulled back with a wounded look in his eye. "What is it?"

Annela couldn't look at him. "I'm—I'm scared," was all she could muster, gripping the box in her hands. "I'm sorry." Somehow they said good night, and she slunk into the apartment, wanting to kick herself. When the door shut behind her, she leaned against it hard. The little package still rested in one hand, the pink ribbon now smashed. She opened it and found a charm hanging from a gold chain, two interlocking hearts. Guilt-ridden, she put it around her neck in front of the hall mirror, blurred vision notwithstanding.

She had to stop pushing him away, but how could she ignore that horrid feeling of fear?

* * *

At work the following week, Annela thought she saw Tommi beneath the blue stairs that led to the fourth floor just in front of The Candy Bag. At the same time, his calls became more numerous. Sometimes he would insist that she still belonged to him whether or not she admitted it, or say she had broken her promise, or, even worse, threaten to do horrible things to her, Kenneth, or Sister Henderson if she didn't come back to him.

More than once the thought of her courageous Great-Grandpa Matti came to mind, and she began to wonder if he would be ashamed of his descendant's cowardice. No more, she decided. Annela refused to live in Tommi's shadow any longer. After work she went straight to Sister Henderson's computer and went online. On the police website she read about a law that went into effect a few years back for restraining orders. She bit her lip as she read about the requirements and procedures. She nodded. Her situation definitely qualified. And it would help reclaim her life. As soon as she could, she would get a restraining order against Tommi.

But she hadn't gotten the chance to start the process when the next morning at work her fears were realized. She looked up from her register and her eyes locked with Tommi's from his position under the stairs. At first she hardly recognized him, standing stiffly with his arms folded across his chest. He hadn't shaved for several days at least, and his hair hung in greasy strands. He held a half-empty beer bottle, but looked as if he'd had a lot more than that to drink. His look sent chills up her spine. A crooked grin spread across his face, and he took a step forward.

"Mia," Annela said, reaching for her friend's arm because she couldn't tear her gaze from Tommi across the corridor. "Where's the phone? I need to call security."

Mia searched around for the hand set, but then she looked over at Annela and noticed her staring at Tommi. "Who is that?"

"Someone who won't take no for an answer." Annela finally looked away to find the phone. She picked it up and dialed the number, but before anyone answered, Kenneth walked into the store.

Annela's heart did a leap. She turned off the phone. "Kenneth! I didn't expect to see you here today." Her relief at seeing him equaled her surprise; he hadn't called since she ducked from his kiss last week. She had hoped it was to give her some time, not because he was upset with her.

"Thought I'd treat you to lunch," he said, glancing at his watch. "I know your lunch break isn't for another ten minutes, but—"

Annela looked at Katrina, who knew about Tommi and had noticed him under the stairs as well. "Take the rest of the day off," the manager said. "We'll get by without you today."

"Thanks," Annela said, grabbing her purse from below the register. "I'll see you all later."

She and Kenneth walked out of the store and headed right, toward the outside doors. Kenneth reached down to take Annela's hand, but she kept her white-knuckled grip on the purse strap. Tommi had followed them out of the store, and the last thing she needed was a scene—sure to happen if Tommi saw them holding hands.

Kenneth looked at her. She gulped.

"What's wrong?" he asked.

She knew he was nearly fed up with trying to decode her mixed signals. One day she takes his hand, the next she recoils again. But seeing Tommi brought back the fears she had tried to overcome. Until she had the restraining order in place, she wouldn't feel safe.

"I'm fine," she said. "Where's your car?"

Kenneth gave her a sidelong glance before responding. She knew he didn't believe her, but said flatly, "It's past the buses."

"Hey! Hey you! Stop!" It was Tommi calling out to them as they went through the doors. Kenneth didn't notice. He probably thought it was just a drunk asking for money from someone else. But Annela picked up their pace more quickly.

Her speed made Kenneth take her arm. "Annela, what is wrong?" She kept going and pulled her arm away. She motioned for him to look behind. A confused look crossed Kenneth's face and he looked back, unsure of what he was supposed to see. It took him a moment to recognize Tommi who, with his drunken gait, couldn't quite keep up with their speed. Kenneth nodded with sudden understanding and increased their speed, steering Annela toward the car.

Tommi kept calling out, and they continued to ignore him. Kenneth now had his hand on Annela's back, and he pushed her along so firmly that it took effort to keep up. Kenneth's jaw was set hard, his eyes piercing. He quickly opened the passenger door and locked it behind Annela after she got in. He jumped across the hood of the car and got in, then tore out of the parking lot just as Tommi reached the edge of the sidewalk, still calling out obscenities and ordering them to come back.

As they drove away, Annela's pulse began to slow down. But Kenneth's jaw didn't relax, and he drove faster than he usually did.

"Kenneth?" she said after a while.

"How *dare* he?" Kenneth burst out in English, the first time Annela had heard him speak his native language since meeting him. He seemed unaware of his outburst. A deep breath helped calm him down. Just a few minutes from the mall, he pulled into the chapel parking lot, took out the key, turned to her.

"Are you all right?" he asked.

Annela nodded. "Just scared me a bit, I guess. Not that he would try to—" She shivered. Kenneth took her hand for comfort, but she ripped it away before thinking.

Kenneth's head fell back against the head rest. He gripped the steering wheel and let out a deep breath of frustration. "Annela, you can't let that one day dictate your life. I'm trying to help you, but all you see when I touch you is a monster. I am not a monster. Annela, I am not Tommi."

"I know."

"If I ever get my hands on him . . ." Kenneth looked away and shook his head to calm himself. "We'll think of something to deal with him. But he can't dictate how you live when he's not around. It seems as if he is really with us half of the time, walking just a step behind us, telling you to not trust me."

"I know, and I'm sorry, Kenneth. I really am. It's just that—"

Kenneth's eyebrows raised slightly as though something had occurred to him. He leaned forward and started the car. "I may not be able to do much about him following you," he said, pulling out of the parking lot. "But I can put a stop to one thing. This has gone on long enough." Kenneth didn't say anything else as he drove toward the mission home. He drove past the house and down the hill toward the beach, then stopped the car.

"Take me to where it happened," he said. It was a demand, not a request, and he didn't have to explain what he meant by "it."

Annela hadn't been to Elephant Rock since that night. Her fond memories of the place had been overshadowed by Tommi. She looked over at Kenneth and opened her mouth to protest, but the determination in his eyes stopped her. Instead she stepped forward and led the way, over the guardrail at the edge of the road and down to the beach. They crossed the sand, then went toward the tall grasses.

There was Elephant Rock in plain view. She took a deep breath, then continued walking toward it. She stopped on the path before stepping onto the rock and noticed fist-sized stones strewn about, maybe the ones Tommi had used to hold down the picnic blanket that fateful day. Annela pointed to the ground before them where the rock melted into the shore.

"Right there," she said, forcing back tears that were already forming.

Kenneth gingerly reached out to touch her shoulder, but then pulled back, unsure how she would react. Annela shivered and stepped past the picnic spot and onto the top of the rock, over the elephant's forehead. She looked out on the gentle ripples lapping the base of the stone and tried not to think too hard about anything that had happened there. Although she managed to thrust aside specific images and memories, she was consumed with emotions, as if the rock itself were feeding them into her heart against her will. Kenneth cautiously stepped beside her.

"So this is your Elephant Rock," he said.

Annela nodded, hugging herself. She sniffed.

"I'm sorry." He didn't say for what, but his tone implied so much—sorry that a place with such fond memories was now tarnished, sorry that she had a near miss with something so vile, sorry for her pain. After several moments, he took her by the shoulders and turned her to him.

"What Tommi did, or tried to do, was horrible. No one can deny that. But you cannot let it ruin your life. There are times when you look at me, and I see fear in your eyes, as if you see him. I'm not him, Annela. That's why I brought you here—to face the memory and bring a happier one to this place. Then maybe you can let it go."

Annela closed her eyes tightly. "It's so hard."

"I know. But one good thing came of that day."

Annela's head came up. "Oh? What's that?"

"As I drove you back to the apartment and saw you sitting in my car, so vulnerable, I wanted to comfort you, but didn't know how. That was the day I first knew there was something special about you, and I had to get to know you better. Who knows, maybe it was Grandpa George whispering in my ear from the other side." They both smiled at the reference. The story of their ancestors somehow connected them to each other in a way neither could articulate.

Annela felt the blood drain from her face as her heartbeat picked up its pace. "It has been fun, hasn't it?"

"It's been more than fun," Kenneth said. "That's not what I meant."

"Then what do you—"

Kenneth put a finger on her lips. "When I boarded the plane in April, the last thing I expected during the summer was to find myself caring this much for anyone."

Annela went up on her toes and hugged him about his neck. His arms engulfed her, and she would have been happy to stay there forever. Kenneth reached down and brushed away a stray lock of hair from her eyes, much as Tommi had done so many times, only Kenneth had something genuine in his gaze, not Tommi's charming sparkle.

She lifted her head slightly and looked into his eyes. But this time she didn't see Tommi in them, and Kenneth read no fear in her eyes.

With an eager smile toying at the corners of his mouth, he leaned down and kissed her.

CHAPTER 14

"Tommi did *what?*"

Sister Henderson was as incensed as Annela had ever seen her on hearing about Tommi's latest games. Kenneth inadvertently referred to the incident over dinner one night. At the time, Annela had brushed it off and changed the subject, but when Kenneth left, Sister Henderson prodded, and Annela had to give some explanation.

"That's why I haven't been working this week," Annela said. When Tommi began haunting the store again on the next two working days, Katrina decided that until Tommi cooled off, it might be better for Annela to stay away. Mall security had escorted him away twice.

"And here I thought that you and Kenneth were just spending as much time together as you could before he goes home." Sister Henderson's eyes narrowed, and she poked a knitting needle at Annela. "That Tommi boy better watch it if I ever see him again."

Sister Henderson returned to her knitting, and Annela tried to hide a smile at the image of Sister Henderson swinging her knitting needles at Tommi as he ran down the street away from her.

"It wasn't a big deal," Annela assured her, unwilling to admit how frightened she had actually been at the store that day. "He didn't do anything."

"No, but he could have. And what will you do for work?" She let out a sound of disgust and poked at the sweater she was working on as if it were Tommi.

Annela circled the top of her glass with a finger. "I'm in the process of getting a restraining order against him. But by the time that happens, Katrina will probably have replaced me. I don't have the slightest idea what I'm going to do for a job," she said with a shrug.

Sister Henderson had a sparkle in her eye. "Why don't you go and pursue your dream?"

"My what?"

"Your dream of going to school in the States to finish your master's. Why don't you read over the information you sent for that's hiding under your bed?"

"How did you know about that?"

"When a thick envelope from Utah arrived, I had a hunch what was inside and why you had requested it," Sister Henderson said with a grin. "Now go. Maybe you can get accepted for fall semester."

"But I can't go," Annela protested.

"Why not?"

"Do you want a list? First there's the money—"

"Not a problem. You had excellent grades at the university. I'm sure you can get a scholarship. I hear they're real generous with foreign students."

"And how do I get there? Sprout wings?"

"I will pay for your airline ticket and living expenses as long as you need me to."

"But Sister Hen—"

She raised her hand to stop Annela. "If you insist on paying me back, fine. But I *will* buy your ticket, and that's all there is to it."

Annela leaned over and kissed her cheek. "You're an angel."

"I sure am," she said with a teasing grin.

"All right," Annela said. "I'll go pull out the information they sent. I'll be in my room."

"And I'll let you know when Kenneth gets here."

Kenneth would be there in the next half hour for a youth activity at the church. The leaders had decided to have an American culture day, with Kenneth as their main speaker. He asked Annela to come along, supposedly to fill in any historical details he was unsure of, but really because they spent most of their free time together anyhow.

When Annela went into her room, she closed the door. She needed some time to think over what Sister Henderson had just offered. Maybe she really could leave Finland and go to school in the

States. She tried to remember all the descriptions Kenneth had given about the area. Annela had never seen real mountains, especially arid ones. She knew she would miss the lush pine forests of Finland, but if photographs were any indication, Utah's mountains had a rustic beauty all their own.

Annela reached under her bed and pulled out the shoe box. She hadn't even told Kenneth about it. She began fingering the leaflets, staring hard at the pictures of campus and trying to imagine what the rest of it looked like. One picture showed the famous "Y" on the mountain. She laid aside a small bunch of papers and reached for the next stack, where she found the admission application. This time she looked over the long form, read the essay questions, and pictured what she might write in each of the blanks. Her heart beat slightly faster, but then stopped as she came across the application dates. The deadline for fall semester had passed long ago. The earliest she could be admitted was January.

Annela came out of her room and sat on the couch opposite Sister Henderson. She glanced up in Annela's direction as she reached for her knitting pattern. Her brow furrowed.

"What's wrong?" She tried to smile. "Has BYU disappeared or something?"

"The soonest I can be accepted is January."

"I still say you apply. We'll think of something until then."

The doorbell rang. Annela eagerly went to answer it. She could really use Kenneth's smile right now. But when she opened the door, she didn't get his smile or now-standard hello kiss. He was far more somber than usual, and it was obviously not a good time to tell him of her plans to apply to BYU.

"Are you feeling all right?" she asked as they went down the stairs to the car.

"I've got a headache," was all he said. Annela didn't believe that was the whole story, but Kenneth seemed in no mood to talk, so she backed off, hoping he would open up later that night. Maybe he was nervous about presenting to the youth, she thought. But that didn't seem likely.

They rode to the chapel in near silence, an occasional comment the only conversation to speak of. She watched his profile from the corner of her eye. His jaw was working, and his eyes pensive, as if he were working on a problem. Annela's stomach felt tight, knowing that something was bothering him. Her mind thought of the possibilities: maybe someone in his family was ill. Or he couldn't finish his research for some reason, or maybe she had unwittingly done something to upset him . . . That seemed like the most likely answer, but she had no idea what she could have said or done to cause this behavior. Annela began to develop her own tension headache from worry.

When they reached the chapel, Kenneth parked the car and got out. He was so preoccupied that for the first time he forgot to open Annela's door. She jumped out and caught up with him just outside the chapel doors.

"Kenneth, stop," she said, grabbing his arm. He turned around. His face was pale, his eyes dull. "What is it?" she pressed.

He turned to her as if brought back to reality, but didn't answer. He stared at the ground. She insisted he explain. "What's wrong?"

"I'm fine," he said curtly, then with a single movement, opened the doors and headed inside. She stopped him again in the hallway, but he said, "They're waiting for me in there, remember?"

"And we're ten minutes early. Something is bothering you, and I want to know what it is. I've never seen you like this."

Kenneth looked down the building's one long hall, avoiding her eyes. He let out a sigh, and his voice sounded spiritless as he said, "Okay there is something wrong. But it's nothing you can do anything about."

Annela's heart ached. "Tell me what it is. Maybe I can help."

Kenneth shook his head, still avoiding her eyes. "I'll be gone in less than a week. What's the point in making an issue out of something that won't matter soon anyway?"

With that he headed down the hallway, leaving Annela behind him. His blunt reminder of his departure hit her heart like a brick. All summer she had tried not to think about it, and although she knew it was soon, she hadn't asked what day he was actually leaving. They had both avoided the topic, but now Kenneth had brought it front and center with a vengeance.

During the activity, Annela watched Kenneth speak about his homeland. As he spoke she pictured herself going to school at BYU, walking along campus hand in hand with Kenneth. With a jolt she realized that even if she made it to BYU in January, that wouldn't happen. He would be teaching in Idaho. Somehow in the corner of her mind she had figured that if she went to the States their relationship could continue.

When Kenneth took her home after the activity, it was little better than riding beside a stranger. Kenneth was no longer so bleak, but his conversation was flippant and shallow, as if they were only acquaintances. He kept talking with a lighthearted air all the way up to the apartment door, and never once reached for her hand. She put on a brave face, refusing to cry until she was inside the apartment. She slipped the key in the lock and waited for Kenneth's good-night kiss.

Instead of even a peck, he simply said, "I guess I'll see you later. Bye."

Annela stood there frozen as Kenneth turned around and headed down the stairs, taking them two at a time, as if trying to escape that much faster. She didn't move until she heard the outside door bang shut, sending empty echos through the building. Only then did she turn the key and go inside. She rested her head against the apartment door, eyes closed. Her hand absently reached for Kenneth's necklace, and she fingered the charm. What had happened to make him so distant? What had she done that upset him so much that he wouldn't even talk about it? A tear tumbled out of each eye.

* * *

If Annela had looked down from the apartment window, she would have seen Kenneth's VW bug sitting in the parking lot for a long time. He got in the car and leaned his head back on the seat.

Now what?

Back in April he hadn't expected to meet someone like Annela. He had looked forward to getting some space, having time to think through everything away from home. He half wished he would have attended the Haaga Ward while he was in the country. That way he wouldn't have met Annela and broken her heart. He wouldn't be hurting right now, either, not knowing what to do or how to control the emotions that would not go away.

In the back seat lay the letter he had received earlier that day, the letter that had changed everything. He hit the steering wheel with his fist, then pushed his fingers through his hair and wiped his sleeve across his face.

He loved Annela. He knew that now.

And he had finally gained her trust, had helped her to move on from that horrible day at the beach. But for what? He would be going home in a matter of days, and she was staying here.

They hadn't known each other all that long, he reminded himself. Could he really call what he felt love?

He rubbed at his eyes. A headache was pounding behind them. Reaching into the back seat, he picked up the letter and withdrew it from the envelope. Once again he read the words, trying to sort out the complicated mess of emotions he was feeling and what to do about them.

CHAPTER 15

The following morning Annela rose with bags under her eyes from little sleep. Her face wasn't flushed and swollen for once, because she hadn't cried. She couldn't. Crying would have been a relief. Instead, her head felt ready to explode with pressure. It was Friday—her last day of work. Katrina had already hired a new girl to start on Monday. That was the same day scheduled for the restraining order trial. She had no doubt the order would be granted but wished the whole mess were over already.

What about tomorrow? she wondered. It was Kenneth's last Saturday before going home. Annela harbored a hope that the two of them would be able to have fun together this weekend, but that was unlikely if he wouldn't tell her what was wrong.

Annela looked at her miserable reflection in the bathroom mirror and dreaded going in to work. She hoped Tommi wouldn't come by again. After last night, the chances of Kenneth coming for a surprise lunch were almost nonexistent, and she was reluctant to call security again.

She sat on the toilet lid and put her head into her hands, feeling so alone. She was losing Kenneth. Without her job, she was unlikely to see much of Mia anymore, and Annela would miss that budding friendship. At least she had Sister Henderson, but Sister Henderson couldn't fill the gaping void all by herself. Annela shook off such thoughts and got ready for work.

When Tommi hadn't shown up by lunch, Annela breathed a sigh of relief, although she kept glancing under the stairs for him. She also kept a hopeful eye out for Kenneth, even though she knew deep down he wouldn't be coming.

"You're really quitting?" Mia asked when there was a lull at the store.

"I wish I didn't have to."

"I know," Mia said with a shrug. "It's just that I was getting used to having someone around who appreciates a good french fry as much as I do." Her sad eyes belied her sunny voice. It surprised Annela that Mia cared so much.

"Oh, you won't get rid of me so easily," Annela said, tossing a bag of chocolate at her. "I'll come back to haunt you every so often."

Mia came over and replaced the candy on the shelf. "How about meeting every Thursday for lunch?"

Annela grinned. "Only if we go to the Hansa Bridge window sometimes."

"Of course. We can go to a bunch of different places. Not for the food, but just to make sure Tommi never figures out where we'll be—of course," she said, her voice genuinely playful now.

"Oh, of course," Annela said with a mock-serious nod.

The first thing Annela did when she came home from work was look at the answering machine. No messages for once, which meant that Tommi hadn't called. But neither had Kenneth. She dropped her purse with a thud and sighed, then headed for the kitchen for a drink of water.

"I'll be starting dinner in about an hour," Sister Henderson called from the living room. Annela brought her water into the living room and sat on the couch.

"So what was that big sigh I heard out there?"

Several weeks ago Annela would have colored at that question, but now she only shrugged. "I guess I was hoping Kenneth would call."

"He did, about an hour ago," Sister Henderson said.

Annela's stomach did a flip-flop. "Oh?"

Sister Henderson nodded and consulted her pattern. "He said he couldn't come to dinner on Sunday."

"Oh." Knots twisted in Annela's stomach, and her eyes threatened to mist up. Sister Henderson looked up from her knitting, then placed it in her lap.

"What is happening between the two of you anyway? Sparks all summer long and now—have you two had a fight?"

"No." Annela laughed ruefully and rotated the glass in her palm. "I almost wish we had. At least then I'd have some idea about what's going on. You know as much as I do."

Sister Henderson's mouth pressed into a line. "I hope you sort this out. He leaves on Tuesday."

Annela hadn't known for sure which day he was leaving until that moment. Her heart grew heavier, and her head began to pound.

"It's been a long day. I think I'll go lie down," she said, rubbing her neck.

Annela didn't hear from Kenneth on Saturday, and she didn't dare call him. She told herself that he was really busy, finishing up all his work before heading home. Besides, it was just as well that she get used to not seeing him. Once he left she wouldn't see him ever again, and in the meantime it would hurt too much to see indifference in eyes that had once looked at her with so much more.

On Sunday morning the doorbell rang. Annela gave her hair a startled spray that landed in her eyes, and she froze to wait for Sister Henderson to answer it. If Kenneth was avoiding her and not even coming to dinner, what was he doing picking them up for church? Annela's hands shook, and she had to take several deep breaths to calm herself enough to put on lipstick.

"Hello, Sister Henderson."

Even though Annela knew it was him at the door, Kenneth's voice sent a burst of panicked adrenaline through her. How was she to pretend everything was fine?

"Good to see you, Ken," Sister Henderson said. "It's been a while. Since you couldn't come for dinner, we didn't think you'd come for us this morning."

"I thought I'd take you to church one last time. Remember, I'm the envy of all the men in the ward to be escorting two lovely ladies to church each week."

Annela leaned against the wall and groaned inwardly. He sounded so natural, as if nothing in the world was wrong. Much different than the distracted Kenneth of the other night. But somehow she knew that when she came out of the bathroom, something would be different. If she could only back up the past few months. Had it all been her imagination? Hadn't she seen the look in his eyes as he kissed her?

Lately when Kenneth arrived, he greeted Annela by taking her hand and pulling her in for a small kiss. He wouldn't today, she knew. With a burst of anger, she threw a brush into the sink and gripped the edge of the counter. *What is his problem?* She closed her eyes and took a deep breath. This wouldn't do. Maybe he would be his old self; maybe everything was fine. She took one final breath and plunged out of the bathroom, plastering a smile on her face and hoping against hope that he would reach for her after all.

"Oh, hello, Kenneth. We weren't expecting you."

"So I hear. You look nice today." He made no movement toward her.

"Thank you. I—I'll be right out. I need to get my scriptures and purse."

Annela ducked in her room and closed the door behind her. Her smile faded, and her knees grew weak. She hated pretending they were mere acquaintances, but with Kenneth's odd behavior, she couldn't do much else. Except maybe whack him across the head with her purse and knock some sense into him. She smiled wryly at the image, knowing full well she could never do such a thing. Sinking onto her bed, she thought about Tommi—the old Tommi. More than once he had changed on her, too. Only she had sucked it up and waited for him to come around. But Kenneth was supposed to be different. He *was* different. And she was furious. *Maybe a little anger is a good thing,* she thought as she stood and went out.

Kenneth's behavior didn't change during the drive to the chapel or the first two hours of church. He chatted lightheartedly between meetings, mostly with Sister Henderson, and made a point of making sure Sister Henderson sat between them. Annela wouldn't have spoken to him anyway; she was too upset for that yet—though she was still aware of what he was doing. She listened to every word, watched for any hint of what was going on in his mind. Relief Society was an escape, if brief, and when it ended, Sister Henderson leaned in. "Tell Kenneth I'm taking the bus home."

A rush of panic came over Annela. She grabbed her arm. "I'll come with you."

Sister Henderson gave her a wan smile. "You've been a wreck all morning. Ask him what's happening in that heart of his. You'll regret it if you don't." She gazed into Annela's eyes. "You do want to talk to him, don't you?" Annela nodded mutely, her eyes watering. Sister Henderson patted Annela's hand. "I thought so."

A couple of minutes later Kenneth's head appeared around the door, and Annela could tell he was searching for them. She replaced her fake smile and raised her hand so he could find her. His eyebrows arched in curiosity when he saw her alone.

"Where's Sister Henderson?" he asked when she approached him.

"She decided to take the bus home." Annela switched her scriptures into the hand nearest his so it wouldn't be dangling awkwardly when Kenneth didn't take it.

"Oh . . . Then I guess it's just the two of us."

"Yes, I suppose so."

They headed toward the doors. "I'm sorry," Annela said offhandedly. Kenneth didn't stop, but looked at her questioningly. "For—?"

"For it just being the two of us. I know you'd prefer it if she were here."

Kenneth started ever so slightly. "'She'? Who do you mean by—"

"Sister Henderson," Annela said, taken aback by his reaction. "Who did you think I meant?"

"No one. Never mind." Kenneth headed for the car with a determined step. She followed half a step behind, trying to keep up. Kenneth didn't say anything as he started the car and pulled out, nor did he speak as they headed down the road. The silence was worse than uncomfortable, and although her mind was full of questions, Annela struggled to voice them. As they pulled into the apartment parking lot, she thought of Sister Henderson and the interrogation she'd give Annela when she came in. She had better at least try to clear the air. Her heart pounded so hard she could hear each beat. It was all she could do to speak before Kenneth reached for the handle of his door.

"Wait."

He froze, then removed his hand from the handle. He didn't say anything, just looked at her, which made it that much harder to go on. She swallowed hard.

"I know you're leaving on Tuesday, but before you do, I have to know what's wrong. And don't tell me that there isn't anything, because I know you better than that. You've been pulling away and I want to know why."

"It's complicated," Kenneth said slowly, avoiding her eyes.

"Have I done something to hurt you?" she asked. *Because you've hurt me.*

"No, you haven't," Kenneth said, looking up, his eyes shiny. "Trust me on that one. You haven't done anything."

"Then what is it? Did I imagine that we were more than friends all summer?"

Kenneth took what felt like an eternity to answer. When he spoke, his voice was hoarse. "It's not as if this can go anywhere. A few days from now we'll be an ocean apart."

To Annela, they might as well already be. Kenneth looked away. "Is there anything else you want to ask?" he said.

There were hundreds of things she wanted to know, but he wasn't giving real answers, so there was little point in asking anything. "No, I suppose not," she said. This was hardly the conversation she had expected to have. "I'll just let myself out."

She opened the door and got out, but before she shut it, she ducked lower to see him better in the car. "Will I see you again?"

He was taken aback. She could tell the thought hadn't even crossed his mind. "I don't know. But I'll call before I leave."

"I'll talk to you then."

Annela shut the door. Sister Henderson would be waiting to hear about their conversation, but all Annela could really tell her was that she had talked to him. She knew nothing more than before.

Her eyes stung as she remembered Kenneth's words. He hadn't denied any feelings, but he hadn't admitted them, either. Had she kidded herself all summer that Matti rescuing George was no coincidence? That there was a reason she and Kenneth had met this summer? Unless the purpose was something different. Kenneth had certainly helped her through her troubles with Tommi. But she wanted the reason to be more than that. She turned around and watched the car pull out of the parking lot, just in case it was the last time she'd see him.

CHAPTER 16

Kenneth is leaving tomorrow morning.

As Annela left the courthouse, she shook her head and tucked the thought in a dark corner of her mind. Why was she thinking of Kenneth at a time like this? She had finally dealt with Tommi, put him behind her.

He had looked better today than he had in months, clean shaven, and wearing a brand new suit and tie. In spite of his clean-cut appearance, Annela had enough evidence and two witnesses—both Sister Henderson and the mission president's wife—who testified about Tommi's behavior and convinced the judge to issue the restraining order.

And she had finally finished everything needed in her BYU application, including an essay and letters of recommendation from two of her former teachers at the university. She had it all in her purse, ready to be mailed off. Annela waited at a bus stop and took a deep breath. With the order in place and her application complete, her life was finally moving on. Her past with Tommi needed to be put on the shelf once and for all.

After getting some lunch, she spent the rest of the afternoon looking for a new job. But no one wanted to hire her when they heard of her plans to move in four months. At least, she hoped an acceptance would come and she wouldn't be around after the new year, so she planned accordingly. On the other hand, school was expensive, and she needed to save as much as possible.

Annela kicked off her shoes by the door and noticed the answering machine's blinking light. As she headed toward the kitchen for a drink of water, she absently pushed the button to hear the messages, pleasantly aware that Tommi wouldn't have left one this time.

"Hi. This is Ken."

Annela froze midstride, then ran back to the phone as if Kenneth himself were there. "Didn't know if I'd get a chance to see you again before I left, so just in case, I thought I'd call with my address in the States so you can write me. Thanks for everything."

He hadn't addressed Annela or Sister Henderson, but he had called himself "Ken," something he never did around Annela, and he'd used the Finnish plural form of "you." He wasn't meaning just her. She replayed the message so she could jot down the address. How convenient for him, she thought as she tucked the note into the edge of the mirror. He didn't have to go out on a limb to write. If she wanted to correspond, it was her move first. She pulled the paper back out and crumpled it in her hand, but before throwing it into the trash, she changed her mind and smoothed out the wrinkles. Sister Henderson would want the address. And maybe Annela would send him a Christmas card. Maybe.

She returned to the kitchen just as Sister Henderson came in, staggering beneath a load of electronic equipment and books, grunting with each step.

"Do you need some help?" Annela asked, rushing over to her.

"Yes, actually. Take those books off the top. I can handle the recorder by myself."

Annela removed four thick books off the top and followed Sister Henderson into the living room, where she plopped it all onto her bed. "There it is," she said, pointing to the equipment with satisfaction.

"There what is?" Annela asked.

"Your new job."

"My what?"

"I was thinking about how hard it is to find work these days. And I hate the idea of you working in public anyway, even with a protective order against Tommi. I happened to mention the problem to a friend of mine who works for the blind library. And *she* happened to be looking for help, and here we are!"

Annela still had no idea what her friend was getting at. "And I will be . . . ?"

"Recording books on tape for the blind."

Annela picked up one of the hardbound books and read the title. The shortest word on it was *anthropology.*

"Not exactly leisure reading, is it?" she said, picking up another, thicker volume.

"No, not really. These are textbooks. But the best part is that you'll be paid nearly two hundred marks for each hour of completed tape. My friend says it takes more time than you'd think to get one usable hour, but even so, that's more than you were making at The Candy Bag, and without ever having to leave the apartment!"

It really did sound quite good. Not particularly exciting, but it was exactly what Annela needed. She put an arm around Sister Henderson, who was beaming with pride over her idea.

"Thank you. This means a lot to me."

* * *

Kenneth stood outside Sister Henderson's apartment. He hesitated before ringing the bell, his hand going to his pocket and feeling the envelope inside. He took a deep breath and pushed the button.

"You'll have to redo that part," he heard Sister Henderson say. A moment later the door opened. He could hear a recording of Annela's voice from the other room.

"Hello, Sister Henderson."

The recording suddenly jumped in volume, sending Annela's voice blaring through the apartment. He could see her in the living room as she searched for and then pressed a button. The recorder stopped. Obviously, his arrival had surprised her. Did she want to see him again? He wouldn't blame her for not wanting to, not after how he had treated her lately. He wondered if he shouldn't have come after all. But Annela deserved an explanation.

"I left that message earlier today when I didn't think I'd make it over," Kenneth said. "But here I am to say good-bye to the best cook in Finland."

"Annela must have gotten the message. I didn't know you had left one," Sister Henderson said, then padded down the short hall and peeked into the living room. "Annela, it's Kenneth. He came to say good-bye."

"I'll be right there," he heard Annela say.

He had the urge to rush into the living room and hold her, but instead he followed Sister Henderson into the kitchen. She began rummaging through her fridge.

"Here it is. I knew I had more *kiisseli*," she called in triumph as she pulled out a pot. Kenneth went to the cupboard to get some dishes when a voice spoke behind him.

"Hello."

He whirled around, his stomach jumping into his throat. "Annela. Um, hi. Come join us for *kiisseli*." Their eyes locked, and Kenneth swallowed hard. Her eyes were filled with emotion. He would have given a lot to know which one.

Sister Henderson motioned toward the bowl in her hand where she had ladled some of the soupy desert. "There's plenty."

"I'd love some," Annela said, taking a seat at the table. "I got home just a few minutes before Sister Henderson," she said. "Then we got caught up with—anyway, I didn't get a chance to pass on your message." She took a bowl from Kenneth. Their fingers barely touched, and Annela pulled back as if from something hot. Kenneth sat opposite her, wishing he could erase the look on her face, but knowing he might be making it worse in a few moments anyway.

With two bowls served up, Sister Henderson wiped her hands on a dish towel and set it aside. "Well then. I have a few things to check on in the living room." She backed toward the door. "I'll be back in a few minutes. Help yourself to some more if you'd like."

Annela shot her a pleading look to stay, but Kenneth gave her a grateful smile. They sat awkwardly for a moment, Annela concentrating hard on spooning her *kiisseli*, Kenneth unable to eat. He finally withdrew the folded envelope from his pocket, then fiddled with it for a minute. He cleared his throat.

"I have felt horrible since we talked yesterday. You don't deserve the way I have treated you, and I can't go home without trying to make this right." He let out a deep breath. She wasn't looking at him. His stomach twisted as he went on. "This might help." He opened the envelope and removed a letter written on delicate pink paper.

Annela took it from him gingerly, looking wary of opening it. As she read the curved writing aloud, Kenneth's knee bounced up and down nervously, and he scarcely breathed.

"'My dearest Kennie,'" she began. "'When we said good-bye at the airport in April, I made the biggest mistake of my life. I was frustrated, and now I regret what I said. Two years just felt like a long time without getting married, so I decided it was time to move on. But with you gone for the past few months, I've come to realize what it was I threw away. I miss you so much. I only hope you'll give us one more chance.'" She lapsed into reading the rest silently, which Kenneth had practically memorized. The author reminisced over their time together and promised she would be at the airport when he returned. It was signed, "'Your one and only, Sherrilyn.'"

Annela's hands trembled as she handed the letter back to Kenneth. He tried to read her face. "Well?" he said.

"I'm not sure what to say." Annela finally looked into his eyes, then back at the tablecloth.

Kenneth leaned forward, wanting her to understand. "When I arrived here in April, I thought Sherrilyn and I were over. I needed a friend, and I found one in you. I didn't expect to find more than that. You've got to believe that I wasn't leading you on, that I didn't expect to feel . . ." His voice trailed off, and his eyes burned. He folded the letter and put it aside.

"Do you still love her?" Annela asked.

Kenneth's head came up, and his throat grew tight at the pain in Annela's eyes. But he nodded. "I think so." He looked out the window, then shrugged. "I don't know. We've been together so long I hardly know what I think or feel about Sherrilyn anymore. But I owe it to her to go home and find out."

Annela nodded. Her lips pressed into a thin line to keep her emotions under control.

Kenneth reached for her trembling hand. "I meant what I said before, Annela. I do care a lot about you. But we've only known each other for a matter of months and now with this letter . . ."

"I understand." In spite of her efforts, a few tears tumbled down Annela's cheeks. She tried to smile through them. "Sherrilyn is a lucky woman."

Kenneth felt as if his heart had been torn in two pieces. He had known this would be hard. He just hadn't realized how hard. Still holding Annela's hand, he stood, and she followed suit.

"I'd better go," he said, glancing toward the door, then back at her. Before they released hands, their eyes met. He drew her close and held her tight. When he pulled back, he brushed her cheek with his lips. But before he could turn away, Annela reached up and pulled his face to hers to give him a final kiss. He returned it, wishing it didn't mean the end. They held onto each other for a moment, then Kenneth pulled back and wiped her wet cheek with his thumb.

When they went to the entryway, Sister Henderson came into the hall to say good-bye, and Annela made one final wipe at her teary eyes. Sister Henderson's eyes sparkled with a thin layer of moisture, and she dabbed at them, but her smile was as broad as ever. Kenneth put on his shoes and jacket, then gave Sister Henderson a big hug.

"I'm going to miss you," he said.

"You mean you're going to miss my food."

Kenneth chuckled. "I won't lie. I will miss your cooking. But I really will miss you too." He turned to Annela. How could he say good-bye?

"I wrote down your address," Annela said, her voice quiet.

"Will you write me?" Kenneth asked.

"Do you want me to?" she asked. Kenneth nodded. "Then I will."

"Then I guess this is it," he said.

"I guess so."

Kenneth paused for a moment, unsure what to do next. He wanted to kiss Annela one last time, but he didn't feel he had the right to anymore. Annela put out her hand. But he couldn't say good-bye with a handshake. He took it, but then pulled her in for a hug. She held him tightly.

"Thank you for everything," Annela whispered into his ear. "I'll miss you."

"I'll miss you too."

They released each other, and his hand lingered for just a moment in hers before he walked away.

CHAPTER 17

At first Annela's new job seemed ideal. She never had to leave the apartment, which meant she never had to look over her shoulder to see if Tommi was following in spite of the order, and she earned good money. But halfway through the first book, she was dying to talk to a person instead of a machine, to speak thoughts and feelings and not a bunch of textbook mumbo jumbo. And although she felt safe in the apartment, she also felt like a caged animal.

She waited for Thursday as if it were parole day, when she and Mia went out to lunch. Not that she couldn't have left the apartment on other days. But she didn't have all that many places to go, and even fewer people to go anywhere with.

Thursday was the first day since Kenneth left that Annela bothered to put on anything fancier than sweats and do more to her hair than pull it back into a messy ponytail. She actually put on a blouse and slacks and curled her hair. She met Mia at the restaurant in City Market, a department store close to the mall.

"What happened to you?" Mia asked when Annela arrived.

"What do you mean?" Annela looked at her clothes, wondering if her slacks had a stain on them or her hair was poking out in six directions.

"No amount of makeup can hide those circles under your eyes."

Annela smiled wanly and tried to change the subject. "It's been a long week. Let's get a table."

But Mia didn't give up. As soon as they had placed their orders, she began digging. "You might as well tell me about it, because I'm not going to stop pestering you until you do."

"It's not that big a deal, Mia."

"Right. And you put blue eye shadow under your eyes. You've listened to me vent more times that I can remember. It's your turn." She sat back, folded her arms across her chest and waited, eyebrows raised.

Annela sighed in surrender. "Fine." She could tell Mia the bare bones of what had happened to satisfy her curiosity. "A week ago Kenneth came over to say good-bye, which was less than pleasant. Then I got a job—"

"Wait a minute," Mia said, leaning forward. "Is Kenneth that cute American who used to come by the store?" Annela nodded and tried to go on, but Mia interrupted. "And he came to say good-bye before going home?"

Annela nodded again. "Anyway—"

"And that was a bad thing?"

"He came over to apologize for some things he did. Turns out he has a girlfriend at home."

"The dog!" Mia sat back in disgust, arms folded across her chest.

Annela waved her hand back and forth. "No, he's not. She broke up with him before he left. They weren't together over the summer. But now she wants him back."

Mia's posture relaxed. "Does *he* want her back?"

Annela shrugged and rotated her glass in circles. "He doesn't know, but he says he owes her another chance." She sighed. "It's just so frustrating. At one point I had even thought that . . . never mind."

Mia's eyebrows furrowed. "That what?"

"That he might be the one to take me to the temple."

Mia looked up from her food, apparently remembering what that meant from Annela's explanation earlier that summer. "Oh, Annela. I'm sorry." She reached across the table and took Annela's hands. "I wish he could have been the one. Does a man have to be a member of your church to do that?"

Annela nodded. "And, as you can imagine, there aren't a whole lot of eligible single men in Finland with that status."

"I'm sure you can find someone to marry in the temple."

"But I don't want to marry just 'someone.'" Annela ripped a roll into tiny pieces as she verbalized what she had only recently admitted to herself. "It's just that—I love Kenneth. I wanted to marry him. I still want to. But he's there and I'm here."

Mia looked pensive. "If I were you I'd just give up on the whole temple thing and find someone here."

Annela shook her head. "It's not something I can just 'give up.'" She started to cut her chicken.

Mia stirred the ice in her glass with a spoon, her brow furrowed. Several minutes and half a chicken breast later, she was still silent.

"Are you going to eat or just watch your ice melt?" Annela asked in an attempt to lighten the mood.

Mia threw down her spoon and looked at Annela with frustration. "Why is it that you have such strong convictions about everything?" She began counting off on her fingers. "You don't smoke, you don't drink, you were constantly reading that scripture book of yours during breaks at work. You go to church *every* Sunday and sometimes during the week for who knows what. And didn't you say once that your church asks you to pay a tenth of your pay? Not to mention that you starve yourself at least once a month. And now this temple thing. I don't understand why you stick with such a demanding religion. And to top it all off, even when you're upset you have that—that *thing* that I don't have. Frankly, it's starting to get a little irritating."

Annela laughed heartily for the first time in ages. It felt good. "I've told you before what it is, Mia. It's the gospel. I have answers that I never had growing up. Not only do I know God loves me, but I know His plan."

Mia poked the peas on her plate. She gazed at Annela as if sizing her up, trying to see what she was made of. "Let me see that scripture book of yours. I assume you still carry it everywhere." She held out her hand and wiggled her fingers for the book, almost daring Annela to prove her wrong. Annela tried to hide the smile creeping onto her face as she pulled the Book of Mormon from her purse. She always carried it around—just in case.

"Here," she said, handing it across the table.

Mia flipped through it for several minutes. She stopped here and there at verses Annela had marked for Mia's benefit. When she reached Moroni, where his promise was marked, Annela pretended to be engrossed in her meal.

Mia closed the book with a sigh and handed it back over the table. Annela pushed the book back toward her. "It's yours."

She was taken aback. "But this is your book. I can't take your holy book."

"I have another copy at home. I want you to have this one. Read it."

Mia wasn't sure how to react. "Thanks," she said, setting it by her purse.

"Will you read it?"

"Sure."

"No, I mean *really* read it. And pray about it. Ask God if it's true, and He'll tell you."

Mia looked skeptical, but Annela pressed her. "Look. You've spent how many years chasing after an elusive something and never finding it. I'm telling you, this book has what you're looking for. Isn't it worth a few weeks of reading and prayer to find out if I'm right?"

Mia smiled. "Okay, I'll read it. Really."

* * *

Kenneth drove to Sherrilyn's condo without really focusing on the road or controlling the car. His mind was absorbed with other things.

Like how much had happened over the last four months, since he had last seen Sherrilyn. He remembered her words at the airport so clearly they might as well have been seared into his brain.

"It's been two years, Ken," she had said. She reached up for the lapels of his coat and held them tightly. She ran her painted nail along the edge of his collar. "I've waited a long time, hoping you would come around. But I see now that you aren't ready for a commitment. And I need one."

Kenneth was stunned. He had thought they were doing fine. Sure, being away for the summer would put a strain on their relationship, but it wasn't anything earth-shattering—he hadn't thought so, anyway. "What are you saying?"

Sherrilyn stared at his chest. When she spoke, her voice trembled. "I'm saying that I need a ring or my freedom."

Kenneth glanced behind him at the metal detectors, where he would be heading in only a few moments. His head was spinning. "What brought this on? Can't this wait until later?"

"How much later? Another year? Two? I've been in limbo for too long. I can't stand another four months of not knowing where my life is headed or whether you are going to be part of it." She looked up, her eyes glittering. "Maybe it took this trip of yours to force us into a decision."

Panic leapt into Kenneth's throat. What could he possibly say right now, in the few minutes he had before boarding? "I'll call you as soon as I get there, in the middle of the night if you want so we can talk this out."

Sherrilyn shook her head adamantly. "After two years, if you don't know that we should be together, then a phone call across the ocean isn't going to change anything. *Do* you know it?" Her eyes implored for the one answer he couldn't give. He needed more time to think, but she refused to give it. And if he didn't go down on one knee right now, would he lose her forever?

She took his silence for an answer. With a nod, she wiped a tear away. "I see. I guess I have my freedom then. Good-bye, Ken. It was a wonderful two years."

She reached up and kissed his cheek, lingering for just a moment. He sucked in his breath and reached to pull her close, to protest, to say something—anything—to change what she had just said. But she spun around and ran across the large room and out the doors.

He still remembered the horrible pain of that moment as her high heels clicked into the distance, her purse jouncing on her hip as he called out to her. He always wondered if she didn't hear him or just didn't come back.

What had been his problem back then? Was it fear of commitment like she said? At the time, he simply couldn't get himself to buy a ring and get down on one knee for Sherrilyn. But it hadn't been so many days ago that he had thought of doing those same things for Annela.

Annela. Kenneth grunted and changed the radio station to something with a heavier beat. This was not the time to be thinking about her. He needed to focus on Sherrilyn right now, decide what he felt and give them one more shot.

He pulled up at the curb next to Sherrilyn's apartment and killed the engine. With shaky legs and a heart beating overtime, he made his way to her door and rang the bell. While he waited, he adjusted his tie. They would be going to a choir concert at BYU, so he had dressed in his suit. Now it felt restrictive, and he wished he could unbutton the collar; it felt so tight. When the door opened, he held his breath until he saw Sherrilyn's roommate on the other side.

"Hi Mindy," Kenneth said. "Is Sherrilyn here?"

Mindy nodded. "She'll be right out."

He kept his eyes busy by looking at the pictures on the walls—there was the one of the Savior with little birds that had always been one of Sherrilyn's favorites. And the smaller one by the same artist that he had given her last Valentine's Day. Tucked into the frame was a picture of the two of them at a BYU dance. That night felt like a lifetime ago.

He heard a noise behind him and turned. On the other side of the room stood Sherrilyn. He caught his breath at the sight. A new dress, dark green and fitted, flattered her narrow waist. The v-neck showed off the small emerald pendant that he had given her for her birthday. Her dark hair framed her face, where she wore the most beautiful smile he had ever seen on her.

"Wow," he said. "You look great."

Her smile widened and she stepped forward. "Thanks. You don't look too shabby yourself."

He put out a hand, and she took it. They drew close and hugged tight. He breathed in her long-familiar perfume and finally relaxed. This was something he knew. This was comfortable. For the first time since landing in the States, he felt at peace. They pulled apart just enough to share their first kiss in over four months. It felt warm and natural, like putting on a familiar coat.

"I've missed you," Sherrilyn said in his ear after pulling apart. "I can wait a little longer if you need the time . . . If it means we'll be together."

Kenneth didn't answer except to hold her tighter and revel in how natural it was to feel her form in his arms.

She was taller than Annela, slightly skinnier, he noticed.

The thought just jumped into his head. He closed his eyes to shut out the comparison. Sherrilyn deserved his full attention. He owed her that, after all they had been through.

"Let's go," he said, and reached for her hand. Together they walked to his car. He opened the door, and before getting inside, Sherrilyn leaned in close and pecked his cheek.

"I'm glad you're back," she said.

* * *

After the concert they went to the Brick Oven, where they had gone on their first date. It was Sherrilyn's idea, and Kenneth had to admit that it was a good one. Sitting only two booths away from the one they had occupied so long ago brought back a slew of memories and feelings, and somehow all their baggage and disagreements dissolved into the background.

They both ordered the famous house root beer, and they shared a garden pizza, deep dish. And they talked like old friends, as though they hadn't broken up at the airport in the spring, as if they hadn't been apart all summer.

It wasn't until they left the restaurant and Sherrilyn suggested they go on a walk that Kenneth began thinking about the summer. They couldn't forever ignore those months. As they strolled down a nearby street past the Elms apartment complex, Sherrilyn shivered and wrapped her arms around herself. Kenneth took off his suit jacket and put it around her shoulders.

"Thanks," she said, pulling the jacket close, then reaching for his hand.

They walked in silence for a minute, when Sherrilyn began the conversation that Kenneth had been trying to start.

"A lot happened over the summer," she began.

Kenneth murmured in agreement. Flashes of memory went through his mind—the Castle of Finland, Seurasaari on midsummer night—and those moments when Annela had been so vulnerable, like the time he picked her up from the mission home. Did she ever think of those days? Probably not. He knew he had hurt her by withdrawing after he received Sherrilyn's letter. Talking about it afterward helped, he knew, but she might not ever forgive him. And he couldn't blame her. He hoped Tommi was leaving her alone.

Sherrilyn coughed uncomfortably. "I met someone over the summer," she said, then looked over for his reaction.

"You did?" Kenneth said, half relieved that he wasn't the only one, half jealous of whoever the guy was. And a tiny bit hurt that she could move on so easily.

She nodded and plowed ahead. "I wasn't looking for anyone. Heaven knows I was such a basket case that the last thing I wanted was to date anyone. Mindy kept trying to set me up, and I finally agreed to go on a blind date with a guy named Chad."

They plodded on, the only sound their steps on the sidewalk and the occasional car passing by. "Go on." Kenneth encouraged her with a squeeze of her hand. He had an irrational urge to hear the story. Who was this Chad person and had he hurt Sherrilyn? Or had she dumped him?

"We went to a play together—*Into the Woods*. I had never seen it before, but Chad had, and he wanted to see how they could pull it off in the round. The witch had this bright red hair, and was amazing. And—" She stopped and laughed. "I don't know why I'm yammering on like this. I guess it's just hard to tell you about it."

"I understand," Kenneth said, and knew he really did. How was he supposed to tell Sherrilyn about Annela? He couldn't deny the feelings he had had for her, but should he reveal them to Sherrilyn?

"Anyway, long story short, we ended up dating most of the summer. He was great fun to be around, but he was too bossy and self-willed and . . ." Her voice trailed off, and her step slowed. "He wasn't you. And I finally realized it wasn't fair to him for me to keep seeing him while the whole time I was wishing I was with you."

They had stopped walking now, and Sherrilyn grasped both of his hands. "It's always been you, Ken. Let's just do it."

"Do what? You mean get married?"

Her lower lip was drawn under her teeth, and she nodded with excitement. "Breaking up was the biggest mistake we've ever made . . . or I guess I should say *I* made. And after being apart for so long, I know what I want. And that's you. Can't you feel it, too?"

Kenneth sighed. In some ways, this was the same conversation they had at the airport. What was his problem? Why wouldn't he just say okay and get engaged? Tonight he felt a slight irritation that she kept pressing the matter. It was the one thing he didn't like about Sherrilyn; she tended to push him into things, make decisions for him. Once she even attempted to change his mind about what to study for graduate school. But through it all, he knew she loved him and sincerely wanted what was best for him—for them.

He turned, she followed, and they resumed their stroll. "Let's not rush into anything," he said.

"I don't think two years and counting is rushing into anything," Sherrilyn countered.

"I mean rushing after all we've been through this summer. Don't we both need some time to work through it, to get reacquainted?" *I know I do,* he added mentally.

What would Sister Henderson say if he could talk to her now? He had her phone number, but of course he wouldn't dare call for motherly advice about something like this, especially when Annela was as likely to answer the phone as the elderly *mummo*. What would life be like if he didn't ask Sherrilyn to marry him? *Or rather, if I accept her proposal,* he added with a glib smile.

"What's so funny?" she asked, noting his expression.

"It's nothing. I just realized that twice now you've all but gone down on one knee and popped the question yourself. Are you sure you still want me to have that job?"

"Are you saying you'll take it up?" she countered.

"It's under consideration," he said with a laugh.

CHAPTER 18

By October Annela had recorded all the books Sister Henderson had brought home and was working on another set. To keep from falling asleep recording, and to keep her voice from cracking, Annela would read each morning for an hour or two, then break to dress and eat breakfast. After three more hours of recording, she ate lunch. Then, if she could stand it, she would read some more. By then her brain was little more than jelly, so she would abandon the recorder and talk with Sister Henderson, help her make dinner, and otherwise try to spend the rest of the day without looking at the address tucked into the frame of the hall mirror.

Annela half-anticipated, half-dreaded, the arrival of the mail. She was waiting for a response from BYU, but she also harbored a wish that Kenneth would write to tell her what had happened with Sherrilyn.

One day in October, Annela finished reading another textbook right before lunch. She turned off the recorder and stood to stretch her legs, then headed for the kitchen to refill her glass with water and get something to eat. She paused by the hall mirror, the crumpled paper with Kenneth's address still tucked into the edge.

Will you write to me? He had asked. *I'll write,* she had promised. But more than a month after his departure she still hadn't put pen to paper. He and Sherrilyn were probably in the middle of wedding plans by now. She downed the last of her water in one gulp and reached for the address. *Just get it over with,* she thought. *Send a letter so I won't have to feel guilty for not writing.*

She sat at the desk in the bedroom and pulled out some paper and a pen from the drawer. "Dear Kenneth," she began, then stared at all the blank space on the rest of the page. What could she say to fill it up? A sheet of scratch paper next to her was soon filled with doodles.

"I've finally been called as a visiting teacher," she wrote, then tried to think of any ward news and the latest doings with Sister Henderson, which only filled the first half of the page. She didn't trust herself to go into anything more personal. Annela glanced at the calendar to remind herself what had happened in the last month.

She told him about the wedding she and Sister Henderson helped bake for. She mentioned a date with Mika Lehto, although she didn't elaborate—like how the hero in the movie they'd seen reminded her of Kenneth. She didn't say she missed him. And she struggled with how to close the letter until she simply signed her name.

Two weeks and another textbook later, Annela had yet to receive a reply. Considering how long it took for mail to get to and from the U.S., it was a little early to expect one, but that didn't stop Annela from feeling frustrated. Why hadn't she thought to ask for Kenneth's e-mail address?

Lunch with Mia was days away, but Annela had to get out. She decided to take a walk and write a letter to her mother, who she hadn't seen in two months. She would have liked to go down to Elephant Rock, but not when it held such a combination of intense memories for her, both old and new. She turned the other way and headed north. Several minutes later she crossed the busy road and climbed the street. She passed the familiar apartments and kept going to the top of the hill, where her old elementary school stood.

The two-story building seemed far plainer than it used to. She always remembered the blue window frames rather than the concrete gray box of the rest of the school. Class had already let out for the day, so the playground was deserted. Annela walked up the ramp, running her hand along the wood railing until she reached the landing where the ramp turned and went up to meet the upper floor.

When she reached the top she looked around the covered area where she used to jump rope and play games when it rained. She turned and gazed over the playground. There were faded paint lines of the games she had played, and long wooden beams on one end of the playground. She and her classmates used to play a balancing game in teams on them. Annela leaned against the railing and imagined her classmates lined up on the beams, trying to knock each other off.

At the far side, a short wall divided the playground from the school medical offices. Annela remembered a small fourth-grade girl sitting on the wall, feet dangling, trying to be brave—until the new boy came and asked to play with her. Tommi had been a lifesaver then.

Annela walked down the ramp, then across the playground to the wall and hoisted herself onto it. She felt so alone and wished that another friend could show up and make things better. She pulled out a pen and notepad to write a note to her mother. She was grateful her mother hadn't come back to the store, as Annela would have worried about her going home and upsetting her father. But she wished she still had a job her mother could visit. Annela missed her more than ever now that she knew her mother loved her, something she hadn't known the first time she had sat on this wall.

"Dear Mom," the note began. Annela had no idea what to say. She wanted to see her mother's face, give her a hug, look into her eyes. *So why shouldn't I?* she thought. The apartment was just a little way down the street, and her father would be at work at this hour. He would never know. School was over for the day, so Kirsti would probably be hanging out with friends. *Mom is likely to be home alone.*

Annela made her way to the apartment building. Heart beating in anticipation, she went inside the building and headed up the stairs. As she reached for the bell, her father's voice boomed on the other side of the door, followed by a crash. Annela fumbled with her purse, found her old key, and opened the door. It swung open with a bang, and she rushed inside, half surprised at her own daring to do so. Her father's fist was raised, and her mother sat cowering in a chair.

"Dad, stop it!"

Oskar turned around, stunned at first by his daughter's sudden appearance. Without a word, he moved toward Annela with surprising speed. He grabbed her shoulders, throwing her toward the wall as if she weighed no more than a dog. She crumpled to the ground with a cry. He kicked her in the stomach and ribs. Jolts of pain shot through her body. He grasped her hair, struck her face, then threw her into the corridor.

The door slammed shut.

Annela couldn't move. She didn't know how long she lay there. She was aware of her mother's cries turning into screams for her sake. Annela wanted to go in and stop her. She would only make him more angry. But the yelling quieted down, and Annela tried to get up. Her father always stormed out to drink after a fight. If he found her lying there . . .

Annela managed to hobble down the stairs, despite the pain in her side. She walked to the far side of a tree, where she collapsed on the ground to regain strength. She hoped her father wouldn't notice her when he came out. Breathing alone sent pangs through her body, and she figured she had a bruised rib or two.

Not two minutes later the building door crashed open. Annela closed her eyes and held her breath, listening to his heavy footsteps come nearer and then fade. He cursed his way toward the street, walking with swift strides. Annela realized that her mother was still there, probably hurting worse than she was, so she rose gingerly and turned back to go inside.

"Mom, it's me, Annela. Are you all right?" she asked after opening the apartment door. When there was no response, she went in. She expected to see her mother crying in a huddled ball on the couch, but instead her feet stuck out behind it. "Mom!"

Annela rushed around to find her mother unconscious with bright red marks all over her arms and face. Some were already starting to swell. Annela's throat constricted, and when she noticed a bloody eye, she stifled a gasp. But her mother was breathing, and there weren't any critical injuries that she could tell. She picked up her mother and carried her into the bedroom, where she woke up.

"Annela, what are—"

"Shhh." Annela reassured her, placing her on the bed. "Are you all right?"

Her mother nodded and tried to sit up. "I'm fine."

Annela urged her back down. "You rest. I'll go get the first aid kit."

Her mother nodded, but as Annela rose to leave, she grabbed her daughter's arm. "I don't need an ambulance."

"I know."

"Don't call the police."

Annela sat back down next to her mother. "But Mom, he has hurt you so many times and he's not going to stop—"

Helena's hand rose to cover Annela's lips. "Don't. This is my choice."

Annela reached for her mother's hand. "But I can't sit by and let him keep hurting you. He's never made you pass out before . . . or has he?"

"It doesn't matter, Annela. Just trust me on this one. It's not as if calling the police would do any good."

Annela didn't know how to react. "How can you say that? Of course it would."

"No, it wouldn't." Helena gave a wan smile. "I know the law. In cases like these prosecution rests with the injured party—that's me—and I won't prosecute my husband."

Annela's heart dropped, but she tried once more. "Will you call me if you need help? If you ever need a place to stay, Sister Henderson would be happy to have you."

Helena patted her daughter's hand. "Thanks. I'll remember that. But promise me you won't call about what happened today."

Her mother didn't seem to have any serious injuries. But Annela couldn't help but think of Tommi. She knew it would probably get worse. She sighed. "Fine. I won't call this time," she said, standing to walk out. Stopping by the door, she turned back. "But Mom, if this ever happens again, I *will* call."

She walked out and closed the door behind her, but before she took a step toward the kitchen, she heard a stifled sob in the other bedroom. Annela pushed the door open and looked inside, where Kirsti sat on her bed, hands over her face. She looked up at her sister.

"It's my fault!" Kirsti cried. Her hair had streaks of orange and bleached blond and her nose was pierced. But it was the black makeup running down her face that stood out the most. On impulse Annela went to her sister and pulled her close, trying not to wince at the pain in her side. They stood there, locked in an embrace.

Kirsti sobbed into Annela's shoulder, saying over and over again, "It's my fault! He found the cigarettes in her purse, but I hid them there. It's all my fault!"

She finally pulled back and wiped at Annela's mascara-stained blouse. "I've gotten your shirt all dirty."

"Don't worry about that," Annela said, sitting Kirsti back on the bed, where they sat beside each other, holding hands until Kirsti's breathing had evened out and she could talk.

"I'm scared, Annela," Kirsti said. Her voice was shaky, and another set of black rivulets fell down her cheeks. "Dad's getting worse every day, ever since he got laid off."

"Dad lost his job?" That explained why her father had been home in the middle of the day. Annela thought back to the money her mother had sent her and wished she still had it to give back. "How long ago?"

"Two weeks, I guess. He's been crazy, Annela, spending money all over the place. Mom says it's to prove that he's not at all concerned about the finances. He even bought a car. It's used, but we still can't afford it. Mom's worried that he'll spend all their savings, and he won't even talk about looking for a new job."

Annela looked at her hands, then back at Kirsti. "Has he ever hurt you?"

Kirsti shook her head, but then stopped and admitted, "Once. But I don't think he meant to. He just shoved me out of the way when they were fighting."

Annela felt sick. He had finally crossed his own line and hurt the child he favored. What line would he cross next? Maybe she should call the police now. But she had promised not to, and she reminded herself that her mother wasn't in any mortal danger right now. Annela knew well enough from experience how scared her mother must be of angering her father even more.

"Why didn't you tell me?" Annela asked.

Kirsti looked up, eyes red. "I didn't think you'd care."

Annela shook her head and held Kirsti's hand tighter. "Why would you think that?"

"For one thing, Mom and I haven't heard much from you since you got baptized."

Annela's own eyes misted. "That's not because I didn't want to keep in touch. It's been so hard not to come back. I've missed you both so much, and I worry about you and Mom every day. That's why I got so excited to see you at the mall that day. I hoped you'd come to see me again."

Kirsti was kneading her hands and didn't look at her sister. "That's the day I realized you didn't hate me."

Annela put a hand on her sister's shoulder. "You're my sister. Of course I don't hate you. I love you."

Kirsti looked up, eyes hopeful. "You love me?"

"I love both you and Mom. And I'm worried about you." Annela pulled out another piece of paper from her purse and jotted down her phone number.

"Call me if you need anything. I mean it. For that matter, I want you to call every couple of days or I'll worry." She didn't say so, but it would be the only reliable way to know when she should call the authorities. Annela already regretted her promise. She wouldn't make that mistake a second time.

Kirsti took the paper and read the number. "I'll memorize it so Dad won't know."

"Good idea. Will you call tomorrow?"

Kirsti was repeating the number over and over when she looked up. " . . . 513. I will."

Annela almost walked out, but Kirsti stopped her with a hug. Annela had to hold her breath to keep from crying out at the pain in her ribs.

"Thanks for coming, Annela. I love you too."

CHAPTER 19

Sister Henderson knew something wasn't quite right. Annela winced when she moved, but refused to discuss it.

They were eating lunch when the mail fell through the slot in the door. Sister Henderson stood to get it, and as usual, Annela did her best to act indifferent. Sister Henderson smiled to herself. The poor girl tried so hard not to be disappointed each day when nothing came from Kenneth or BYU. She scooped the mail off the floor and sorted through it.

"You've got two letters," she said to Annela, a gleam in her eye. A white envelope with a blue logo in the corner dangled between her fingers. "This one looks official."

Annela's hand shook as she reached to take them. She opened the letter from BYU first.

Her face lit up. "I've been accepted for winter semester!" She looked up at Sister Henderson, then back at the letter. "I'm going to graduate school in America," she said in disbelief.

"Of course you are," Sister Henderson said, grinning. She took Annela's hands, pulled her to her feet, and led her around the kitchen in a silly celebration dance. "You did it! You did it!" she sang. She slipped on the rag rug, and Annela tried to catch her from falling, but they both fell down and ended up in a laughing heap on the floor.

"Are you all right?" Sister Henderson asked, noticing Annela wince and hold her side.

"I'm fine," Annela said, standing and holding a hand out. Sister Henderson took it and got to her feet, then straightened her dress and began clearing the table.

"So are you going to open the other letter?" Even she could tell that her voice sounded a little too forced to be casual.

"I suppose I should," Annela said, picking up the other envelope. She set it back down. "But I'll help you with the dishes first."

Sister Henderson raised an eyebrow. "As if I'd let you help when you've got that letter to read. Tell me all about it when you're done. I'll take care of the dishes."

Sister Henderson fully intended to finish the dishes while Annela read the letter, but she was too excited for Annela's sake. She tiptoed to the bedroom door and listened, hearing a deep sigh, followed by the rip of the envelope opening.

Sister Henderson's toe tapped anxiously, and she finally retreated to the kitchen, hoping Annela would tell her what the letter said. Sure enough, a few moments later the bedroom door opened and Annela came into the kitchen. Sister Henderson turned around, expecting to see Annela's smile. But the girls' face was pale and drawn.

"Here. Read this," Annela said. She sat at the kitchen table.

Sister Henderson took the letter and read it silently.

> *It was nice to receive your letter. I apologize for taking so long to respond, but I've been rather busy finishing my dissertation and teaching three history classes. I'm glad all is well for you and Sister Henderson and that you had fun on your date with Mika. He seems nice. I hope Tommi is no longer bothering you. Tell Sister Henderson I miss her kiisseli and Sunday dinners. Hope to hear from you soon.*
> *Best regards,*
> *Kenneth Warner*

She looked up from the letter. "'Best Regards?' I don't know what to think." She handed the letter back to Annela. "I wouldn't have thought Kenneth could write something so—"

"Impersonal? I didn't think so, either. I reread it twice, hoping I had missed something. This could have been to a virtual stranger, not to someone . . ." Annela waved away her emotion "What did he mean with that comment about Mika? He's probably hoping something will happen between us." She tossed the letter aside.

Sister Henderson picked it up. "I say you write back and give him a piece of your mind. I assume you already asked about Sherrilyn." Annela shook her head and Sister Henderson asked in exasperation, "Then what *did* you say in your letter?"

"Not much."

"Land's sakes, child, ask him about Sherrilyn. If you don't ask, don't complain if he doesn't tell."

"I can't ask him. This is his way of avoiding the topic. If there's something he wants to tell me, he will. Otherwise I can assume they're together, and I would just be interfering in his life." Annela stormed out of the room.

Sister Henderson held the letter. "At least answer him," she called after Annela, who turned back.

"I'll try. But not today." She put her shoes on, grabbed her jacket, and left.

Sister Henderson pursed her lips together. She eyed the letter, then the door, and the letter again. "If she won't do it, I will." With determined steps, she went to the living room desk and started a letter to her favorite missionary. "I know I promised not to meddle, Annela," she whispered under her breath. "But sometimes a body must do what needs to be done."

* * *

Over the course of the next week, Annela tried to write to Kenneth a few times, but each time she would start telling him personal things or referring to something they had said or done during the summer, so she tore up the letters. After all, his heart belonged to someone else now. He wouldn't want to hear about what was happening in hers.

Sister Henderson had conspicuously taped his envelope to the mirror, and it worked; Annela felt a pang of guilt.

"Fine. You win," she called into the living room as she untaped the letter from the mirror. "I'll answer him."

But instead of writing a letter, Annela pulled out the postcards Kenneth had bought her at the National Museum. A postcard didn't have much space to fill. She picked the one with Väinämöinen and Aino and for the first time related to both characters. Like Aino, she had run from Tommi, but now, like Väinämöinen, someone was running from her.

"I thought I'd send you a reminder of your last trip to the National Museum," she wrote on the postcard.

Sister Henderson's voice called from the other room. "Send him my love."

"I will," Annela said. Sending Sister Henderson's greetings nearly filled the rest of the space. She wished him well and mailed it.

Annela still looked over her shoulder for Tommi, although he hadn't yet directly violated the order. Even so, once she thought she'd seen him near the apartment building. She hoped he would soon accept that she would never be his, with or without the order.

Thursday and lunch with Mia came again. When she got to the mall, Annela found Mia leaning against the staircase that Tommi used to stand by. Since Mia was engrossed in a book, she didn't see Annela approach. Annela leaned down to look at the blue cover to be sure. The Book of Mormon. Annela smiled and greeted her.

"Oh, hi," Mia said, slipping her bookmark in place and closing the book quickly, as if Annela hadn't seen it. She noticed Annela's pleased look. "Yes, I'm finally reading it," she said as if defending herself. "I promised I would, didn't I? I thought it was about time."

"What do you think of it so far?"

Mia paused, as if searching for the right words. "I'm not sure," she finally said. "I don't understand all of it."

"Neither do I. But I understand a little more each time I read. I'll be learning from it for the rest of my life."

Mia picked up her bag, and Annela followed her absent walk around the corner and down the long hall past the escalators. "The strange thing is that even though I don't understand what I'm reading half the time, I don't want to stop reading. Katrina has been making fun of me, because that's all I do on my breaks now. She said she wonders if it's a disease, first you and now me, and who'll be the next to catch it at The Candy Bag." They both laughed. Mia processed her thoughts as they passed the escalators and turned the corner that led to the Hansa Bridge.

"I can't describe it, Annela. It's just—well, peaceful. I wish I could always feel that way, but it goes away almost as soon as I stop reading. I almost went nuts one day when I didn't have time to read. I stayed up late that night just to feel calm enough to sleep. Weird, huh?"

"Not so weird."

"Then what is it? That Holy Ghost thing you told me about?"

"Yes. And when you get the *gift* of the Holy Ghost, it'll always be there, so long as you're living worthy of it."

Annela stopped at the Hansa Bridge food window and suddenly realized the two of them hadn't officially decided where to eat. "Do you mind eating here?"

While they ate, the conversation turned to other things. Annela avoided any reference to Kenneth, but told Mia about the rest of her life, how she and Kirsti were now on good terms for the first time since she could remember, how she finally had contact with her family several times a week when Kirsti called.

"Do you mind if I come to church with you on Sunday?" Mia asked as they threw their trash away. "Just to see what it's like, I mean."

"Not at all," Annela said, trying not to look too pleased. "And I'll introduce you to some friends who can teach you more about it."

They headed back toward The Candy Bag. When they reached the store and Mia turned to say good-bye, Annela had to ask, "Out of curiosity, how far are you into the Book of Mormon?"

Mia colored slightly. "I'm in Mosiah . . . my second time through." She looked at Annela warily. "I really am weird, aren't I?"

"Not at all, Mia. Not at all. I'll see you Sunday."

* * *

On a Saturday afternoon, Kenneth drove to his mother's home in Shelley for a visit, thinking about Sherrilyn and Annela the whole way from BYU—Idaho. Why did things have to be so complicated? He wished his life were like a video rental, that he could just skip this part, see how the story turned out without having to go through it

He parked out front and crossed the front yard, then walked in, the screen door banging behind him.

"Kennie? Is that you?"

"Hi, Mom," Kenneth said as he took off his jacket and closed the door behind him.

"I'm in the study," his mother called.

The study was his late father's office, which his mother had recently converted into her hobby room. Shelves, storage containers, and cubbyholes were filled with scrapbooking supplies, and work tables lined the room. On the far side, his mother sat with paper and photos sprawled out on the table in front of her. When he entered the room, she swiveled around in her chair and opened her arms. "Come here and give your mother a hug," she said.

He obliged and pulled up a folding chair. "What are you working on?" The photos weren't the usual spread of grandchildren or family reunions, or even the album his mother had been working on in honor of his father. These photographs were all black and white, and several brittle, yellowing documents lay in piles as well.

"Your Grandma Peterson's ninetieth birthday is coming up," she offered in explanation.

"That's right," Kenneth said, remembering. "Is Aunt Judy still planning that big reunion?"

His mother nodded and turned back to the table. "That's why I'm doing this." She gestured toward her newest scrapbook project and reached for a photograph. "Look at this."

Kenneth took the photo and studied it. The two people in the front row were obviously parents, surrounded by their—Kenneth counted quickly—ten children. The first on the left, a girl who looked ten or so, seemed familiar.

"Is this one Grandma Peterson?" Kenneth asked, pointing at the round face with the rosebud mouth.

"That's right," his mother said. "And then there's Mildred and Calvin and . . ." She strained to remember all the siblings' names and then slowly listed them off. "And of course, in the middle, there are your great-grandparents, Maria and George."

At the name, Kenneth tensed and studied the face of his great-grandfather. His mother continued, but he hardly heard her.

"I wanted to do something special for Grandma. She's the last living sibling in her family, you know. She'll be the oldest one at the reunion. I thought it would be neat to have a scrapbook of her family." She stopped talking, but when her son didn't respond, added. "Kennie? Are you all right?"

He broke his gaze and smiled at his mother. "Of course. I'm fine. Grandma will love the scrapbook. Are you—" He tried to sound casual about the question he wanted to ask, though he felt suddenly emotional over it. "Are you going to include anything about Great-Grandpa George and the mine?"

"Of course," his mother said, taking the picture from his fingers. "I have a layout planned for it. Doris Thurgood—you remember her from the ward, don't you?—did some research for me and found some newspaper clippings about it—even some information from the centennial memorial."

Kenneth chewed the inside of his lip and nodded. "Are there any pictures of him and the man who rescued him?"

"I wish," she said, turning to the front of the scrapbook. "Here. Look at what I've done so far."

Kenneth looked over his mother's layouts with her. But while usually he could appreciate all the effort and detail she had put into her pages, this time his mind was elsewhere, and he kept stealing glances at the photo of Great-Grandpa George lying on the table above the album.

He tried to imagine Matti Heikilä, what he might have looked like. Did he have a dark beard like George? He had risked much to come to America and seek his fortune. But that risk almost cost him his life when he rescued George. Was the risk too much, was that why he had gone home? Kenneth wondered how well George and Matti knew each other before the disaster—if Matti had saved a friend or an acquaintance, and how that had come to bear on his decision to risk everything. How *did* he make that choice? And did he regret ever leaving the safety of Finland?

Kenneth wondered what George and Matti would say if he could ask them for advice right now. George had always led a safe life. Matti had made both decisions when a lot was at stake. The two men stood in his mind on two sides of a fence, and Kenneth felt as if he had to pick a side to stand on.

On one was Matti. If Kenneth picked that route, he would be taking a huge risk. He would give up a woman he knew almost better than himself for the excitement of learning to understand Annela, though he had known her for only a few months and in a completely foreign environment. On the other side was George, who, after the mining explosion, had abandoned his life of independence, and grudgingly returned to work at his father's side, forever tied to the land. He chose to sacrifice his dreams for a safer vision of the future. Kenneth knew that down that path lay the known and safe territory of Sherrilyn—his comfort zone. No risk, but nothing ventured either.

He wished he could speak with both men right then and ask if their decisions had been worth it, exactly how each man had made their life-changing decisions, and whether he wished he had acted differently.

But there was no getting that kind of counsel, and it was up to him to decide.

"Did I ever tell you in my letters that I met a woman in Helsinki? She . . ." His voice trailed off, and he couldn't go on.

"You met someone?" The decorative scissors his mother was using clattered to the table, and she stared in shock. Kenneth had almost forgotten how his mother viewed Sherrilyn as a daughter already. This was not a place he could look to for counsel either.

"She's a descendant of Matti Heikilä, the man who pulled George from the mine," Kenneth finished, his throat tight.

His mother relaxed, clearly relieved, and added a pop dot to the back of the accent she had just made. As she adhered it to the page, she went on. "What a coincidence! I wonder if she has any pictures of him."

Kenneth murmured something to change the subject. He could hardly get himself to write Annela in the first place. Asking for a favor was out of the question, even if it was for his grandmother's scrapbook.

Kenneth stood and kissed his mother's cheek. "I'll go get something for dinner. Does Arctic Circle sound good?" He left the house and drove down the quiet Shelley streets, in a haze as images of the fence came back—Annela and Sherrilyn on both sides, asking him what he was going to do.

* * *

Mia not only came to church on Sunday, but agreed to attend the missionaries' American Halloween party they were planning for the English class later that week. When Mia and Annela arrived, Elder

Stevens shoved two smoking paper cups in their direction. He had a drawn beard for a "costume," since he couldn't really grow one during his mission.

"It's root beer," he said in response to their wary faces. "An American drink."

"Why is it smoking?" Mia asked, looking into her cup suspiciously.

"It's just dry ice. It won't hurt you," he assured them. "It took us a week to find a place that sold it in Helsinki. Trust me. It's good." Mia thought the root beer tasted no better than cough medicine. Annela finished hers to be polite, but didn't ask for seconds. During the first part of the evening Mia had a hard time turning off her flirting reflex around the elders. Annela had to remind her more than once that missionaries couldn't date.

The elders had decorated the stage for the party and managed to talk one of the mission president's daughters into posing as a mummy. Her toilet-paper-wrapped self lying on a mock tomb was the first thing guests saw when they went up the stairs to the stage. On the far end of the stage, a plank of wood was suspended between two ladders. Hanging from the wood were doughnuts hung on strings. Elder Stevens ushered the English class students to the doughnuts. Elder Harper, newly transferred to Marjaniemi, waited for them to line up so he could give the instructions. He had slicked-back hair and wore a black cape. His Dracula costume was finished off by a pair of fake teeth.

"Everyone stand in front of a doughnut," he instructed them, the fake teeth muffling his words. He removed them. "Sorry about that. Can't talk with these in. Everyone line up, one doughnut per person."

Everyone did as they were told, and Elder Harper went on. "The rule is that you must eat the doughnut without using your hands."

The sound of hurried feet and doors opening and closing sounded. Everyone turned their heads toward the door, where Elder Densley headed to see what the commotion was about. Meanwhile, Elder Harper began the contest. Annela's doughnut swung back and forth, and she couldn't get hold of it with her teeth. Mia had taken a hearty bite out of hers and chewed as quickly as she could.

They heard a muffled voice from the hall, followed by someone coming up the stairs. At the sight of Sister Henderson, Annela straightened, her doughnut forgotten. The contestants stopped and looked at Sister Henderson, whose knuckled hands gripped her coat and purse. She panted, and her hair was windblown.

"There you are, Annela," she said, catching her breath.

Annela hurried into the hallway, her heart beating hard from Sister Henderson's wild-eyed look.

"What is it?" Annela asked, afraid something had happened to her or the apartment.

"I couldn't reach you on your cell phone for some reason, so I came here as fast as I could." Sister Henderson reached for Annela's hands as if to steady her. "Kirsti just called from the hospital." She paused as if trying to find the best way to say it. "Your parents and Kirsti have been in a horrible car accident, Annela. Your mother is in the hospital, but she has a lot of internal bleeding, and the doctors aren't sure—" She stopped, then added quietly, "Your father didn't make it. I'm so sorry, Annela. So sorry."

Annela tried to grasp what she had just heard as Sister Henderson led her trembling frame down the hall to the chairs between the bathroom doors, where they sat down.

"How?" Annela finally asked. Her voice sounded as if someone else were speaking.

"Your father was drunk. Drove the wrong way down a one-way street into an oncoming car."

"And my mother?"

"They don't know yet."

Annela couldn't comprehend it. She felt as if a numb chill had come over her, preventing her from feeling anything. "But Kirsti is all right?"

"She'll be fine. She broke her arm and has some bruises. She's still at the hospital. I told her I'd come for you."

"She needs me." Annela blindly headed for the door, but Sister Henderson had the presence of mind to go tell Mia that they wouldn't be back.

They found Kirsti sitting on a chair in the hospital hall, waiting for news from the doctors. Her left arm was in a cast, her face ashen except for scrapes above her left eye and on her cheek. The dim lights outlined her huddled silhouette, her good arm wrapped around her as if she were trying to hold in the tears that coursed down her face. Without a word, Annela ran to her sister, dropping to her knees, where Kirsti fell into her arms with a wracking sob.

"Oh, Annela. What are we going to do?" she cried into her shoulder.

"We'll be all right," Annela said, holding her tight.

"What are we going to do?" she asked again.

"I don't know."

Sister Henderson let a nurse know they had arrived while Annela stayed with Kirsti. They sat for so long they lost track of time. Neither said much as they clung to one another for strength and waited. At Annela's insistence, Sister Henderson finally went home. Shortly after that, Annela and Kirsti were asked to identify their father's body. Kirsti refused to come, so Annela went alone.

His face was so disfigured that Annela almost didn't recognize him. But his thick eyebrows and the mole on his neck were familiar enough.

She nodded, then turned away. "It's my father."

The technician pulled a sheet back over his face and made a move to leave.

"Do you know the details of the accident?" Annela asked suddenly.

The technician turned back. "Are you sure you want to know?"

Annela nodded firmly. "I'm sure."

He consulted some notes. "According to the police, his car was old and didn't have an air bag. And he wasn't wearing a seat belt. He went right through the windshield. If it's any comfort, he probably didn't suffer."

Around midnight a doctor came down the hall to Annela and Kirsti in the waiting area. She rubbed her eyes as if they had been strained for hours. "Are you the Sveibergs?" she asked. Annela nodded. "I'm Dr. Hiltunen," she continued.

"How is my mother?" Annela asked.

Dr. Hiltunen ran a tired hand across her forehead. "Stable for now. It'll be touch and go for several hours still. She bled a lot from a lacerated liver. It looks as if she had several minor lacerations on her liver from previous injuries, and the accident nearly burst it. For some reason she is also quite bruised around her neck and has a broken nose, even though she was wearing a seat belt."

Dr. Hiltunen hesitated, as if not sure how to approach her next thought. "Was your mother—I mean, did your father ever—"

"He beat her all the time," Kirsti said bluntly. "He hit her the other night in a fight."

The doctor nodded.

"Doctor, are you saying that's the reason she is in such bad condition?" Annela asked.

Dr. Hiltunen grimaced. "I can't say for sure, but it is a definite possibility that with a healthier liver she would be doing better."

Annela got a pit in her middle. If only she had called the police that day at the apartment, maybe she could have prevented this from happening. Then again, she herself had refused to see Tommi's problems until it was almost too late. She probably wouldn't have been able to convince her mother to leave or prosecute. She shook her head to clear her thoughts as Kirsti spoke.

"But she will be all right, won't she?"

"I don't know," Dr. Hiltunen said honestly. "It's too early to tell."

"Can we see her?" Kirsti asked.

"Not yet, but soon, I hope." Dr. Hiltunen looked at them with sympathetic eyes. "Why don't you two get some rest?"

"Not until I see her," Kirsti said.

"I'll let you know as soon as you can."

Kirsti and Annela returned to their seats to wait. Somehow Annela managed to be the strong one. But she knew it was only because she hadn't allowed the reality of the accident to sink in. She had to be strong, for Kirsti's sake. She would deal with her own feelings later.

As the minutes dragged on, Annela didn't sleep, although Kirsti finally collapsed on her shoulder. Some time later, the hollow sound of footsteps came down the corridor. Annela tried to move her arm, but it had fallen asleep from the weight of Kirsti's head. Her eyes felt bloodshot, her stomach heavy, as if it were lined with lead. Dr. Hiltunen appeared.

"Annela?"

Kirsti woke up at the sound. "Can we see her now?" She scrambled to her feet. Annela reached for Kirsti's hand and held it tight for support.

Dr. Hiltunen shook her head with fatigue as well as sympathy. "I'm sorry. Your mother passed away about ten minutes ago."

Kirsti's hand flew to her mouth. "No!" She wrapped her arms around her sister's neck so tightly it hurt Annela. "She's not dead!"

"It's all right, Kirsti. It's all right," Annela said, stroking her hair. She felt as if she were watching the scene, detached. For Kirsti's sake she couldn't fall apart. The longer the reality took to sink in the better, and later the pain would come.

When they were brought to the room, Annela expected Kirsti to run in and throw her arms around their mother, but instead she stayed by the door, gulping back sobs, eyes half closed as if she couldn't bear to look on the sight.

Annela stood by the bed where the doctors had tried to save her mother's life. Tubes and monitors were all over the room. The hospital staff must have removed the tubes from her mother's body after she passed away, for which Annela was grateful.

She gently took a lifeless hand, and the strong front she had put up melted away. Emotion overpowered Annela as she held her mother's hand against her cheek. She kissed it and cried shamelessly.

"I love you, Mom. I'm so sorry I didn't call." If her father hadn't beat her mother, she would probably be squeezing back and smiling now. "I hate him!" Annela whispered vehemently.

No sooner had the words escaped her lips than a strong but gentle chastisement came to her mind, as if her mother were standing behind her with a hand on Annela's shoulder.

"Do not say such things," the voice said. "Do not harbor bitter feelings. I have forgiven him, and you must too. Do not grieve, Annela. I am home."

CHAPTER 20

Annela tried to be strong for Kirsti, but despair crept through the numbness a few times as it had in the hospital, and more than once she and Kirsti cried in each other's arms. Neither had any idea what to do as far as a funeral was concerned. Sister Henderson and the Relief Society made most of the arrangements, even though neither of the girls' parents had been members. Annela figured her mother would have wanted an LDS burial, and now that he was on the other side, she could only hope her father would change and accept the truth as it was taught to him there.

The funeral was on a bleak November day. Clouds threatened a storm, but a dark haze was all they brought to the sky. Only a few centimeters of snow covered the ground, although it was already quite cold. The long hours of summer light had gone with the warm weather. Days grew dark much earlier now, Annela noticed glumly.

Annela and Kirsti each laid a rose on the pine coffins, which rested in front of the handful of mourners. The sisters didn't have many living relatives, only their mother's two sisters and their children. Since their parents had lost contact with any friends Annela and Kirsti knew of long ago, they hadn't known how to get in touch with any. Annela looked across the caskets at her aunts and their families. She hadn't seen most of them for years, ever since her father's tirades had gotten out of control and her family had stopped visiting relatives. Annela wondered if her Aunt Liisa still hosted the Christmas party every year.

The bishop dedicated the graves, and it was over. Everyone headed back to a reception building on the cemetery grounds for a light meal. Kirsti and Annela took up the rear and were some distance from the graves when Annela realized she had dropped her scarf.

"Go on ahead," she told Kirsti as she headed back. "I'll catch up."

Annela retraced her steps, scanning the lightly flaked ground for the brown cloth. Instead of her scarf she found a tall, older man dressed in black. They both started in surprise when they saw each other.

He held a single white carnation which he was about to place on her mother's coffin.

"Oh, excuse me," he said. "I thought everyone had left. I didn't want to intrude." He turned to duck into the trees.

"You didn't intrude," Annela said. He stopped and turned around slowly. "I just came back to find my scarf."

"Is this it?" he asked, pulling it from his coat pocket.

"Yes," Annela said, curious as to who this stranger was and why he held her scarf. He handed it over, and she wrapped it around her neck. "Thank you."

"Are you Annela?" he asked.

"Yes," she answered warily.

"I thought so." He smiled. "You look a lot like your mother. You're very pretty."

"Thank you, Mister . . . ?"

"Hesanto. I'm just an old friend. I wanted to pay my respects." He placed the flower on top of the blooming mound already on her mother's coffin, then awkwardly excused himself. "It was really nice to meet you, Annela." He ducked under a low-hanging pine branch and disappeared in the thick trees of the cemetery.

* * *

When it was all over, Kirsti and Annela had the overwhelming job of sorting through a lifetime of belongings and deciding what to do with them. After digging through some boxes in a closet, they discovered that their mother had been a sentimental pack rat. Even though Annela had learned more of her mother's love over the past several months, it came as a surprise to her that she'd kept papers from Annela's earliest years at school. One box held some old report cards, pictures of Annela holding newborn Kirsti, and a necklace she had made for her mother when she was just six. Annela fingered the necklace and smiled.

For the first time since their parents' deaths, she and Kirsti smiled and laughed at all the "remember whens." Annela brought two more boxes from the hall closet, handed one to Kirsti, and opened the other.

"Hey Annela, look at this!" Kirsti held up a stack of old textbooks, much older than theirs, which their mother must have kept from her own school days. Kirsti also found several old diaries. Annela went through a box that held old pictures, many black and white, mostly of relatives she didn't know. Some had names below them, and she recognized a handful of the faces in them, including her grandparents and an aunt. At the bottom of the box was a thin album with black paper that she almost missed. She pulled it out and flipped through the pages. Several photos had fallen off their places and didn't have names on the back, so Annela had no idea who most of the figures were. She had never seen the album and wondered when it was last opened.

Toward the back, Annela noticed aging paper folded in half. It looked stashed there, almost hidden. Curious, she opened it up.

"Hey, Kirsti, look," she said, pleasantly surprised. "I found my birth certificate."

"And I found my first-grade picture. Look at my teeth." Kirsti held up a picture of a little blond girl with curly pigtails and both front teeth missing. Annela almost held up the paper for Kirsti to see when one of the names caught her attention. The line labeled "Father" read "Mikko Hesanto."

Annela reeled back and stared in shock. Then, just as suddenly, it all made so much sense. It was almost as if a curtain had been pulled back from the cobweb-covered years, and suddenly she understood her life.

"So he was right," she murmured with a smile. "Dad really had no Mormon daughter."

"What?" Kirsti asked, thumbing through one of the diaries.

"Nothing," Annela said. She looked at the album where the yellowing paper had rested for so long. Another paper sat there, too, a note addressed to her mother.

Helena,

Enclosed is a small Christmas gift for your Annela. I figured Oskar must know she's not his, and won't want me to have anything to do with her, so please don't mention this to either of them. I simply had to do something, even as small as this, for her.

A picture was pasted into the album on the same page—a smiling little girl with a Christmas tree in the background. Annela didn't remember the picture being taken.

"Hey Kirsti, can I see some of those diaries?"

"Sure. Here's one when she was in *Lukio*, and this one—"

"Is there one when she's older? Maybe my age?"

Kirsti opened a few and looked at dates. She handed Annela three volumes. "These are probably from later on. They were under this one."

"Thanks." Annela took them and climbed onto her father's old chair, something she had never dared do before. Somehow it didn't seem strange, as if she had curled up on it with her father to hear bedtime stories all her life. The smell of cigar smoke almost seemed comforting in its familiarity.

The cover of the first diary cracked slightly as she opened it. She flipped through several pages, scanning for dates. At first she looked for the year before she was born, about three years after her parents married, but stopped early in one volume when she saw the name "Mikko." The entry was a year before her parents even married, shortly after they met.

This is getting ridiculous. At first it was fun having two men fight over me, but the excitement has worn off. At times I'm tempted to toss both of them. They keep telling me I have to choose between them, but at this point I don't dare. Mikko is sweet and kind, and he makes me laugh. We have the same goals—we both want our children to be religious, even though neither of us were brought up that way. But then there's Oskar. Passionate is the only way to describe him. He does nothing halfway, and he is so romantic. He even serenaded me on my birthday last month. Mikko wouldn't have ever thought of doing something like that, even if he could carry a tune. Not that romance and musical talent are any basis for choosing a husband.

Oskar's entire life seems to revolve around me. He is sad when I am sad, happy if I'm happy, and miserable when he thinks he has hurt me. He gets jealous whenever he finds out I've been out with anyone else, especially Mikko, even though I knew Mikko months before I ever met Oskar.

I can't deny that it's all very flattering, and sometimes I wish Mikko showed his feelings more than Oskar does. I have more in common with Mikko, and he's easier to talk to. But then, Oskar has given me flowers several times, Mikko not once. Oskar is easily the better looking of the two, and we have some amazing chemistry, but should that matter? I care for them both, but I don't dare pick yet. Right now I'm leaning toward Mikko, but I can only imagine how breaking it off would crush Oskar. He has already given Mikko a black eye over me. What would he do about an engagement ring? I'd never forgive myself if he seriously hurt Mikko because of me.

Annela read on about her mother's difficult time deciding between her two suitors, and her eventual decision to stay with Oskar. After a year of marriage, the pages of the diary were tear-stained and full of pained entries of her husband's controlling behavior and his first strikes at her. Between those entries were flowery ones describing how he would apologize and make up with her with roses, chocolate, or a new dress.

Annela skimmed the entries for several months, stopping whenever she read either man's name. Helena had finally fled for safety about two years after their marriage. Her parents hadn't believed the stories about her charming husband, the only side of him they had ever seen, so she went to her in-laws for help. When they too sent her away, she sought refuge with Mikko.

I didn't know where else to turn. I didn't even know if Mikko was married yet. I just had to find a safe place. When he answered the door, I fell into his arms and

*wept. I couldn't tell him what had really happened with
Oskar, just that we had a horrible fight.*

After that incident, the diary which had been written in at least every
few days was painfully silent. The next entry was three months later.

> *I have done something horrible. Something I swore to
> God on the day I married that I would never do. It is bad
> enough that I broke one of the most sacred trusts on earth,
> but now another person will have to pay for my sin. I fear
> I am carrying Mikko's child. I do not dare tell Oskar that
> I am pregnant. We have grown so far apart since I came
> home that he will know as well as I do that it could not
> be his child. He didn't know where I had been those two
> days, but I think he has his suspicions. It won't be long
> before I have to tell him. He'll be able to look at me and
> know. I pray God will forgive me and give me strength to
> live with my sin and try to pay for it.*

Annela closed the book and held it tightly. Her entire childhood
and her parents' relationship had been a locked chest that had suddenly
opened up. In knowing the events leading up to her birth, everything
made so much sense. This one family secret explained volumes.

Her mother stayed with a violent man to pay for her sin. The
Geisha bars came each Christmas because Mikko was trying in some
small way to be what he couldn't be otherwise. Her father hated what
she represented, and her mother never dared show affection toward
Annela, the evidence of her betrayal.

So many emotions came over her, all conflicting. On one hand,
she was glad that Oskar wasn't really her father. But at the same time
she was angry that no one had ever told her. By the way her relatives
treated her, they must have known. Finally, a great sadness came over
her for what had never been.

Strangest of all, as Annela continued going through her parents'
belongings, the anger toward her father faded ever so slightly. Now
she understood. Understanding didn't justify a thing he'd done, but
knowing *why* made the pain more bearable.

CHAPTER 21

Kenneth stood at the post office counter and filled out the address on an envelope. His hand shook from nervousness, making his handwriting all but illegible. He retraced the letters to make them clearer, thinking back to Sister Henderson's letters. Annela hadn't written in months, and her last letter was about as warm as her postcard message had been long. All he knew for sure was that she was coming to BYU for winter semester. And that would be his only chance to talk with her face to face.

"There you go," he said, pushing the envelope across the counter. "You're sure it'll get there by the end of the week even with the Christmas rush?"

"We'll do our best," the woman said, which was less than reassuring.

He watched the letter get tossed into a container, and even then he hesitated and wondered if he should try to get it back.

"Next, please."

Kenneth stepped aside to let the next customer in. He plunged his hands into his coat pockets and braced himself against the Idaho winter air.

* * *

Mikko Hesanto stood before his wife's headstone, gripping his hat between his fingers. The brim would never be the same.

"Aino, I wish now I would have told you about her—about Annela, I mean." He shook his head as if to clear his thoughts. "I suppose I should back up. You remember the story about Helena? Of course you do." He looked up and around, making sure no one was watching. This was a private moment. He rarely spoke aloud to Aino. Usually he thought his words. His feet shifted uneasily beneath him in the crunching snow.

"If it hadn't been for Oskar, I probably would have proposed to Helena. Of course, that was years before I met you," he added, as if needing to reaffirm his love and loyalty to his late wife.

"When Helena chose Oskar over me, I never thought I would see her again. But one day, out of the blue, she showed up at my door. We . . . well, let's just say that the next winter Annela was born." His voice grew husky as he confessed the past to Aino. "Helena thought it would be best for Annela to never know about me. As much as I wanted to be part of her life, I agreed. They had their own family, I had no right to invade it. I just prayed that Oskar would see Annela as his own child, whether or not he realized the truth."

He paused, his eyes stinging. Looking around, he noticed a family visiting a grave several meters off, and he lowered his voice. "But now that Helena and Oskar have both passed on, I can't help but wonder if Annela would mind my contacting her. Would *you* mind? I gave my life to you. You know how much I love you, don't you? Of course you do."

He took a deep breath and nodded. "I'll look her up."

He bade Aino good-bye, wiped a thin layer of snow and ice from the words on her gravestone, and tromped away through the dry snow.

On the way back to his apartment, he stopped at a small grocery store, and by the time he stepped out and headed for home, the sun had already faded, and the street lights were turning on. It was so dark even in the afternoon now—and winter wasn't even half over yet, so he might as well get used to it, he knew.

As he approached his apartment building, he saw a young woman standing outside. She looked over the directory, her gloved finger moving along each name, until it stopped at his, then moved to the side and pushed the button next to it.

His heart did a leap as he recognized her scarf. "Annela?" he called.

She looked over her shoulder, her face lined with tension. At the sight of his eager face, she smiled back. "Mr. Hesanto? I didn't think you would remember me from the cemetery."

"Of course I remember you," he said, mentally adding, *You're my daughter. How could I forget you?* But did she know their relationship?

He took out his key and opened the front door. "Would you like to come up? I'm making salmon and new potatoes. I've even got fresh dill."

Annela's eyes lit up. "I'd love to."

She followed him into the elevator, hesitating only slightly at the door before stepping inside and standing beside him. Moments later they entered his apartment and shed their coats and boots. He caught Annela eyeing his wedding picture on the wall.

"My wife passed away three years ago," Mikko said.

"I'm so sorry," Annela said, then moved into the living room. She stopped abruptly when she saw the end table next to the couch. On it was a framed copy of Annela's second-grade picture. It had spent the years tucked away in an old journal, and just last week Mikko decided to get it out, put it in a frame, and display it so he could look on his daughter's face.

"How did you . . . ?"

"Your mother sent it to me," Mikko said quietly, stepping to Annela's side. "It's the only one I ever got. Did you know that I'm . . . ?" His question trailed off as he waited for her answer.

His gut tightened. Would she resent what he'd been to her mother? Would she hate him for coming between her parents? Would she be upset that he never contacted her—except for his measly Christmas gifts? They were so small he figured Helena couldn't deny him that much, even if Annela never knew where they came from.

"Did you know?" he repeated lamely, not clarifying did she know what.

But she seemed to understand what he referred to and shook her head. "Not until recently. No one ever told me. After the funeral I found some of my mother's things that explained everything. It answered a lot of questions."

He nodded and continued to look at the school portrait with her, when she added, "And I'm glad you are my father."

"You are?" Relief washed over him, releasing his thoughts. "I have wondered about you all these years. You have no idea how much I wanted to contact you, but your mother and I agreed it would be best for you to have your own family." His thoughts raced; he had so much he wanted to tell her, to ask her, to catch up on. Where could they possibly start?

He offered her a seat, and the two of them sat side by side on the sofa.

"I saw the obituary," Mikko began. "It said only that your parents died unexpectedly. Was it an accident?"

Annela's hands clasped together and she nodded. "Dad was driving drunk and hit another car head-on. He died at the scene, but Mom made it to the hospital. They tried to save her . . . The doctor said if it hadn't been for Dad, she might have survived."

Mikko's brow furrowed. "How is that?"

Annela shrugged. "You must know what my dad was like."

Mikko had no idea what she referred to. "I knew him decades ago, remember. He was just a jealous boyfriend back then."

"Oh," Annela said quietly, then seemed to choose her words carefully. "Dad used to . . . hurt Mom. A lot. And her past injuries from him are probably why she didn't survive the accident."

Mikko felt as if someone had just punched him in the stomach. He could hardly breathe at the thought of Oskar laying a hand on Helena. "How long had that been going on?"

Annela looked up, surprised. "From her journals, it looks like it was almost always like that. In fact, that's why she came to you that day."

Mikko stood up and paced the room, running a hand through his hair. "I had no idea. She said they were having a rough spell, that they had had a big fight, but she didn't say a thing about him hitting her."

He stopped by the mantle and gripped the edge, remembering that day so long ago when Helena came to his door in tears. He remembered—now—that her cheek was bruised. But she had insisted it was from running into the door frame as she hurried out after their fight.

And he had believed her.

He struck the mantle with his fist. "Why didn't she tell me? I wouldn't have let her go back if I had known."

Behind him, Annela spoke quietly. "That's probably why she didn't tell you."

Mikko closed his eyes tightly to ward off the emotion that erupted in his heart. It was suddenly as if he was back at that day, more than twenty-five years before, as if he could save Helena from her husband. The love he had felt for Helena overwhelmed him, returning in full force.

Annela rose from the couch and crossed to him. She touched his arm. "You really loved her, didn't you?" she asked, tears welling in her eyes.

Mikko nodded, then coughed through the tightness in his throat. "I always have." He patted her hand, then looked down at it.

"You have your mother's long fingers," he said, stroking them with his thumb. He looked into her face and smiled. "I'm sorry you have my nose. Mine gets red when I cry, too."

Annela's hand went to hers, and she laughed. Then she put her arms around him and hugged him tight. "I'm so glad I got to meet you."

Mikko clung to her small form. It felt so much like Helena's, he could weep. After all these years, he held his daughter. He wasn't about to lose her from his life again.

"I love you," he said.

* * *

"You're going, Annela."

Kirsti and Annela were bundled in their winter coats, scarves covering half of their faces to keep out the frozen air. It was a bitterly cold December day, and they were heading home from buying Christmas gifts. Annela squinted over her scarf at Kirsti as they left the *kioski* and opened their candy bars.

"I don't know if I can leave you alone without any family."

"I'm a big girl. I'll do just fine with Sister Henderson."

The dry snow squeaked under their boots as they walked, and Annela thought about leaving her sister. Kirsti was right. She was becoming quite a young woman now, and she had abandoned most of her eccentric habits. She had given up smoking and started dressing more modestly—although Finnish winters practically demanded the latter. She had even dyed her hair back to a semi-normal color somewhere between her natural blond and a sandy brown. She hadn't seen her old friends since coming to live with Annela and Sister Henderson, and she had been completely respon-sible with her schoolwork, something Annela had never known her to do. If Kirsti lived with Sister Henderson, she would do just fine without her big sister. But that wasn't the only reason Annela hesitated to leave.

"We're finally getting to know each other as sisters should, and I'm going to mess it all up by leaving," she said. Annela had also just found her father, and ached to get to know him better. They had spent almost an entire day together, but they had just scratched the surface—in some ways Annela had even more questions now. At least they had promised to keep in touch, and perhaps she could learn more through letters than living in the same country.

Kirsti pulled her scarf down to take a bite from her candy bar. She smiled—a pretty smile now that her lips were no longer covered in black lipstick. "It's strange, isn't it? A few months ago I would have thought I wouldn't care if I never saw you again, but now—well, I'm really going to miss you." She chewed on her chocolate for a moment before adding, "But you're *still* going."

"You really want me to?"

"It's what you want, isn't it? You're set to be leaving in a week, Annela. You already have your plane tickets, your housing, your classes. You've already paid your tuition. It would be ridiculous to back out now. Besides, you'd regret it for the rest of your life if you stayed."

As they walked to the bus stop, Annela knew Kirsti was right. While she hated the thought of leaving her homeland and sister behind, she knew it was right for her to pursue an education—and, in all likelihood, the rest of her life—in the States, especially if she wanted a temple marriage. She ignored the image of Kenneth that returned to her mind and tried to think of what her life at graduate school would hold. She needed to go.

When they walked into the apartment, Sister Henderson stood in the living room with a sheepish grin on her face, hands behind her back. Kirsti and Annela removed their coats and boots and went to her. Kirsti tried to walk around Sister Henderson to see what she was holding, but Sister Henderson backed away and shook her head.

"Sorry, Kirsti. This is for Annela's eyes only."

"What is it?" Annela asked, curious but laughing.

"First, I have a confession to make." Sister Henderson motioned with her head toward the couch. "Sit down." Curious, Annela obeyed, and Sister Henderson joined her on the couch, still holding one arm behind her back.

"Remember how I told you to find out what had happened between Kenneth and Sherrilyn?" she asked.

The names sent a jolt through Annela, but she tried to stem her outward reaction. "What about it?"

"You never did, did you?"

"I wrote him a couple of times." Annela picked lint off her pants.

"Yes, but did you ever ask about what happened with Sherrilyn?"

"No. If things went well, they're engaged or maybe even married by now, and his life is none of my business."

"After that letter you showed me, I wrote to him myself and told him my mind."

Annela's eyes flew open. "You didn't!"

"I most certainly did," Sister Henderson said with a matter-of-fact nod. "And I won't apologize for it, either. I told him all about your life and your plans to go to BYU."

Annela's stomach twisted in knots. What if she saw Kenneth on campus? She had counted on him not even knowing she was in the country. The last thing she needed was to have him casually look her up as an old buddy if he came to Provo. Sister Henderson's smile returned.

"Then this morning a letter arrived for you, priority mail." She finally brought her right hand from behind her. Annela's hand moved to finger the charm, which she still wore daily. Her throat dried up.

Sister Henderson handed over the letter, then stood up and motioned for Kirsti to come out and leave her sister alone.

Annela's hands trembled. It had been so long since she had allowed herself to even think Kenneth's name. Now she was bombarded with memories of his face, his laugh, his bearlike embrace. She opened the letter, took a deep breath, and began to read the brief note.

> *Dear Annela,*
>
> *A lot has happened since we saw each other last, but I can't write about it. Letters are so impersonal—I guess we've both learned that recently, haven't we? You meant*

so much to me over the summer that I feel you deserve to
be talked to face to face. Besides, we Warners owe a debt
to Matti's family, right? Sister Henderson told me about
your plans to study in the States. She already gave me
your flight information. I'll see you at the airport.
Until then,
Kenneth

The letter fell to her lap, still in her hand. What did he have to tell her? That he and Sherrilyn were engaged? Married? Would she be at the airport too? Annela's stomach went tight. She would rather not meet Kenneth's first love, but it wouldn't be unlike him to want Annela and Sherrilyn to be friends.

You meant so much to me over the summer, she read again. What did that mean? Was he acknowledging their friendship or something more? Or was he coming to talk to her out of sheer duty because something about their ancestors' shared connection made him feel guilty?

She agreed with Kenneth that letters could be impersonal. Their track record on that point wasn't too good. But at that moment she would have preferred knowing *something,* even from a measly postcard, than to have a long wait of total uncertainty. Her hands trembled as she refolded the letter and put it back into the envelope.

CHAPTER 22

"He said he'd meet you at the airport," Sister Henderson said as she came into the living room.

"I know. And I don't want him to. I'd rather know whatever he has to tell me now." Annela closed her laptop and sighed. "But I can't reach him anyway. His roommate says he's out of town, at his parents', I'm guessing. I looked online for their phone number, but it's unlisted." She absently fingered the charm around her neck. "And I don't have his e-mail address."

The doorbell rang, and Sister Henderson went to answer it. "That must be Mia. She'll help take your mind off it."

Instead of going out together, Mia had taken the day off work to help Annela finish packing and run last-minute errands. But first they had a lunch of Sister Henderson's split-pea soup.

"I can hardly believe you're leaving on Tuesday, and you'll be going to school in another country," Mia said, stirring her soup to help it cool. "I wonder if you'll ever run into Kenneth."

Sister Henderson looked up at Annela from her bowl. "You haven't told her?"

Mia's eyebrows went up. "Told me what?"

Annela let out a breath of air. She didn't enjoy talking about Kenneth's brief and cryptic letter. "He wrote to me, saying he'll be at the airport to tell me something important."

"Did he say what happened with the other girl?" Mia asked eagerly.

"No," Annela said, shaking her head and letting soup drizzle off her spoon back into the bowl. "But I'm guessing that's what he wants to tell me about." She looked up with a pained smile. "Won't that be fun."

* * *

Christmas was bittersweet. Everything they did in holiday prepa-
rations reminded Kirsti and Annela that their parents were no longer
with them. Decorating the tree with Sister Henderson's straw and
wood decorations brought back many memories, all good. Their
father never bothered to stick around to help decorate, so the three of
them would sing along to a tape of Christmas music as they hung
straw pine cones and wood-shaving ornaments.

Helping Sister Henderson create the traditional feast for
Christmas Eve was no different. Kirsti and Annela shared memories
as they helped prepare the multiple courses.

"Do you remember the time Dad bought hot mustard for the
ham?" Annela asked as they peeled vegetables.

Kirsti laughed out loud. "I remember having my eyes water all
night from it."

"Dad warned you not to put so much on."

"I know," Kirsti said, gathering vegetable peels to throw out. "But
I like mustard. I didn't think it would be *that* hot. Do you remember
the Christmas Eve that you burned your hand?"

Annela grimaced at the memory. "I still don't know how I forgot
to put on the oven mitt before taking out the casserole."

The ward missionaries came over for Christmas Eve dinner, and even
Elder Smith, who had just arrived in the country a week earlier, liked the
rice porridge. He got the almond, and Sister Henderson gave him a bad
time about how he would be the next to marry. Poor Elder Smith didn't
know the language well yet, and didn't know if she was kidding until his
companion started laughing and Sister Henderson joined in.

When the elders left, saying it was getting late, Sister Henderson,
Kirsti, and Annela let the mound of dishes wait as they retired to the
living room to exchange gifts. Kirsti and Annela told each other about
when they each realized for the first time that it was one of their
uncles in that Santa suit handing out gifts to the children on
Christmas Eve. They had a lifetime to catch up on.

Sister Henderson gave Annela a beautiful temple dress with lace
around the collar that she had made herself, for use when Annela
would be able to go. Kirsti gave Annela the navy blue sweater she

wanted. When their individual gifts were opened, one small package remained toward the back of the tree.

"What's that?" Annela asked, pointing.

Sister Henderson craned to see. "Oh, that. I almost forgot. It came in the mail the other day. It's for you. I didn't recognize the name or address."

She reached back and brought out the small, oddly shaped package. Annela's name was scrawled across the top in black marker. She tore off the paper to reveal a note taped to four Geisha bars and a box of French pastels. "To Annela. Merry Christmas. Remember to send me your address in the States so I can keep up our Christmas tradition. Mikko."

"Does it say who it's from?" Kirsti asked.

Annela smiled. "An old friend."

* * *

Annela was packing when the doorbell rang and Sister Henderson answered it. A moment later she came into the bedroom, carrying a package of flowers and a large card.

"This came for you," she said.

Annela's eyebrows went up as she left her suitcase. "Who is it from?"

Sister Henderson shrugged. "It doesn't say. You'll have to open it to find out."

Annela placed the flowers on the bed, sat beside them, and opened the envelope. She immediately recognized Tommi's handwriting. Her throat grew tight at seeing his straight, angled script. The protective order had just expired, and since she was leaving, she hadn't seen a point in renewing it. Now she regretted the decision.

> *I wanted to wish you a Merry Christmas. I know
> you have no reason to trust me, but I have something to
> tell you.*

Annela had forgiven him, but that didn't calm her nerves any. She wondered if Tommi were in the hall or standing on the sidewalk watching the apartment window.

I heard somewhere that yellow is the color of friendship. So I sent you a dozen yellow roses. I hope I haven't ruined our friendship for good.

Annela's hand went to the flowers before she continued reading.

I have some serious problems, but I guess you know that. When you got that order against me I got real upset. I couldn't believe you would try to cut me off. And then I heard that your parents died. That news shook me up, and it made me do a lot of hard thinking. After a while I realized that I was ruining my own life, that I was making you unhappy, and that in trying not to lose you, I had pushed you away. I suppose the long and short of it is that thanks to you I decided to go to counseling. I've been going for the past couple of months, for my drinking and abusive behavior.

The last phrase was written in an uneven hand, as if Tommi had a hard time writing the words

Don't worry. I won't be bothering you anymore. Someday maybe you can agree to see me again, but for now I'm just glad I had you in my life. I have a long way to go, but I think I've really changed. I'm not the man who hurt you.

His final words read, *Thank you for keeping me in your heart. Just like you promised.*

CHAPTER 23

Before she knew it, Annela was checking in her bags at the airport. Her flight would be leaving soon, and she needed to say good-bye, but she procrastinated. A few months ago she would have welcomed a chance to leave for graduate school. But as she looked at Kirsti, Mia, and lastly, at Sister Henderson, she teared up.

"I'm going to miss you all so much," she said.

"We're going to miss you too," Mia said. "I can hardly understand your courage, Annela. You're leaving your home, your friends, and the only family you have to go to a foreign country. You're willing to give up everything."

Annela shook her head and smiled. "No, not everything. I would never give up everything."

"I know," Mia said with an understanding nod.

"And I'm really not giving you up," Annela said. "There's the telephone and e-mail, and even visits sometimes." But as Annela said the words, she knew that as soon as she boarded the plane, she would leave a world behind that she would never be part of again. Things would never be exactly the same. And while she didn't want time to stand still, she knew there was always a pang inside when something dear is lost forever, even if it has been replaced by something just as good or better.

Annela took a deep breath and picked up her carry-on. "I guess it's time for me to go."

"Almost." Mia took Annela's arm and looked at Sister Henderson with a twinkle in her eye. "Annela, I finally found what I've been looking for. You were right about where to find it."

Annela's eyes shot open. "Mia, you don't mean that . . . ?"

Mia nodded. "I had my baptismal interview yesterday. I'm getting baptized on Saturday." Mia grinned, pleased to see her friend speechless. Annela screamed and gave her a huge hug. They held each other tight. "I just wish you could be here for it. I'm sorry it didn't happen earlier."

Annela pulled back and shook her head. "The Spirit works on its own schedule, Mia. A week earlier you may not have had your witness. I'm just glad your search is over."

"Me too." Mia's eyes sparkled, her inner beauty greater than anything makeup could create.

* * *

After too many hours in the air, Annela peered out the window and saw the rocky terrain she had heard so much about. There they were—the gridlike layouts of cities, the beautiful mountains, the Great Salt Lake. And although she enjoyed the view, the butterflies in her stomach multiplied by the second. For the third time in the last twenty minutes, she pulled out her cosmetic case, checked her eyes for smudged mascara, and wiped some powder across her face.

The plane finally landed and taxied to the terminal. When the passengers began heading down the aisle, the butterflies turned to a lead ball. What did Kenneth have to say? Her own feelings toward him hadn't changed. What if he brought Sherrilyn with him? That would be more than she could bear. She pushed down the tiny hope that maybe his news had nothing to do with Sherrilyn.

Then again, what if after mailing the letter, he decided not to bother coming after all? That would be almost as bad. She would always wonder what he had wanted to say. The *what ifs* continued to plague her as she gripped her bag on her lap and watched the steady stream of passengers file past.

Some looked tired, as if returning from a long and tedious journey. Others had excited expressions, and she knew they must have loved ones waiting to greet them. Three missionaries in worn suits filed by, and Annela could imagine the excited faces of family and friends they would see. When the line of people thinned, and only a handful of passengers remained on board, she took a deep breath and entered the aisle, her bag slung over her left shoulder.

Annela walked through the tunnel and into the gate, then down the long hallway toward security and baggage claim. She tried to calm her heart as she walked, although it beat so loudly she half wondered if the people walking near her could hear it. Her nerves got to her, and she tripped stepping onto the escalators. On the floor below, past the security checkpoint, she saw family members holding signs and balloons, and someone who she guessed was a girlfriend, waiting for one of the missionaries. The young woman held a present in one hand and with the other wiped her eyes with a tissue. A few steps away from her, a wife and children waited, waving as their father reached them and was engulfed in hugs. In front of Annela was a group of young people with backpacks, probably world travelers on one of many stops.

She reached the bottom of the escalators without seeing Kenneth. She turned around in slow circles, searching the crowd for his face.

"Annela!"

As she whirled around to see him, her heart stopped and felt heavy. She swallowed hard and finally noticed that he was alone. She put on a smile. "Hi."

He gave her a hug, and they pulled back a bit awkwardly, standing in silence while travelers bustled around them.

Annela hefted her bag higher on her shoulder. "You look good."

"Thanks. So do you."

Kenneth shoved his hands into his coat pocket and looked around nervously. "I, uh, I had to come tell you that Sherrilyn and I are no longer seeing each other."

Annela looked up, a seed of hope sprouting to life inside her. "But what about . . . ? You said you loved her."

He nodded. "At one time I did. But I understand now that it wasn't the kind of love that can survive hard times and come out stronger." He took Annela's hands, which began shaking at his touch. All the memories of the past summer came back with a rush.

"Back in April when Sherrilyn dumped me, I was crushed. She had been a huge part of my life for so long. The last thing I expected to do in Finland was find you. From the first day we met, I could see in your eyes you were true to those you called friends, and I really needed a friend. And then I found myself loving you, and knowing for the first time what it meant. I felt as if I knew you better in one summer than I did in years of dating Sherrilyn."

Annela's heart raced. She held her breath as he continued.

"When I got home, I couldn't stop thinking about you. I tried. I even pretended you were nothing more than an acquaintance. Your short letters helped convince me I was right. Then Sister Henderson wrote that you still cared." He clung to her hands, his eyes imploring. "*Do* you still care?"

Annela nodded mutely. "I always have."

Kenneth broke into a smile. "Come over here." He took her hand and led her across the floor, where he stopped on a stone map of the world. He placed her over Finland, and he stood over America. Then he fished into the pocket of his coat for a moment. Annela's brow furrowed slightly, unsure what he was doing, until he pulled out a small box and knelt down on one knee.

As Annela caught her breath, several people in the jostling crowd stopped to watch. For once in her life, she didn't care. Kenneth opened the box to reveal a glittering solitaire. He took her left hand in his right. Loudly, in clear English, he spoke.

"Annela Sveiberg, I went across the ocean and found you. Will you join me in my homeland and marry me?" he said in cheesy bravado.

The butterflies returned, but this time she didn't want them to go away. "Yes, Kenneth. I will marry you, with all my heart."

Kenneth placed the ring on her finger, then pulled her toward him across the ocean and into his arms. Everyone within a thirty-foot perimeter cheered and clapped. Annela's heart felt ready to burst as Kenneth pulled her close and kissed her.

"I'll bet our great-grandfathers are doing high fives in heaven right now," Kenneth whispered. Annela laughed, and he kissed her again.

After retrieving her luggage, they walked to the parking area hand in hand, and Annela thought about all the changes in her life—and in herself. A year ago she hadn't known the Church existed. She had thought her mother hated her, and she had no place but a cold rock by the ocean to call home.

Annela glanced around at the mountains, the airport signs, and the people, and breathed in the smells. Everything should have felt foreign and strange, but it didn't. Kenneth leaned down and kissed her cheek.

Annela was home.

ABOUT THE AUTHOR

Annette Luthy Lyon has written ever since piling pillows on a chair to reach her mother's typewriter in second grade. She spent most of her childhood in Provo, Utah, although during the three years she spent in Finland with her family, she learned to love her mother's homeland.

Many locations featured in the book are ones she spent time at herself, including the elementary school she attended, Elephant Rock, the mall (including, of course, The Candy Bag), Seurasaari, and the Castle of Finland. Sister Henderson's home is modeled after the apartment one of Annette's Finnish friends, Katri, lived in.

A *cum laude* graduate from BYU with a BA in English, Annette has published many articles, including several special projects in association with *Creating Keepsakes* scrapbook magazine. She served on the League of Utah Writer's Utah Valley chapter board for three years, including as president for the 2001–2002 year. She has received numerous awards from the League, including the Quill and Diamond publication awards.

She enjoys scrapbooking, knitting, camping in the Uintahs, reading, and spending time with family. She and her husband Rob live in American Fork, Utah, with their four children.

Annette enjoys corresponding with other readers, who can write to her in care of Covenant Communications, P.O. Box 415, American Fork, Utah 84003-0416, or through e-mail at info@Covenant-lds.com.